Kathy:  A Valley Is Never A Finale

By Michelle Murray

Although inspired by a series of true events, all characters, events and dialogue have been adapted in the process of dramatization for an intriguing fictional tale.

Kathy's earliest memory was of her mother sitting on her for an imagined infraction when she was about three years old. She struggled to breathe and tried to claw her way loose. She began to do the same thing the moment Jake placed her in a playful headlock.

As an athlete, Jake thought of a headlock as a display of love to his sister. Kathy, however, slipped into a dark place for just a moment and thought he had tried to kill her. Jake brushed his wavy black mane out of his piercing green eyes and apologized when he saw the startled look on Kathy's face. He told her he'd see her that evening for dinner. Kathy hugged her brother and told him she looked forward to it.

This was Jake's final year at Dallas' Southern Methodist University, where he was a football player. If all went as planned, he'd get into law school there and have a fabulous career ahead of him. It was doubtful with his most recent knee injury last season that there would be any actual shot at the NFL career he dreamed of.  That was quite all right.  Jake was shocked he still held a spot on the football team.  He had received an academic scholarship, but on a whim, tried out for the football team and made it.  Not only did he make it during his freshman year, he was part of the starting line-up.  He easily proved himself on the field.  He moved the ball down the field with a speed that made Olympians swoon.  His bones, however, defied him. Jake had suffered 17 injuries and 26 missed games during his college career.

Kathy's heart sang when she thought of all the wonderful things Jake accomplished in spite of that. The two of them had been forced to struggle hard in Life.  It finally looked like things were about to fall into place. Kathy had finished college four years earlier and had dreams to become an Army pilot.  The desire to make sure Jake finished college had derailed that dream, at least for a while.

If Kathy had left to pursue a commission at Officer's Candidate School and become a pilot, Jake would have been totally on his own and she was certain he would have never even set foot in a college. Girls and a lack of money would have, no doubt, lured him toward a road that led only to a destination known as Trouble. Though divorced, their parents were unified on one front: Kathy and Jake, their offspring, were inconveniences and annoyances that had served only to disrupt their lives. Once a kid of theirs turned eighteen, they were on their own. No more support, no more guidance, no more anything at their expense or headache. Heck, they really didn't provide these things when the kids were younger either. They produced only venom and a swift attack to a kid that needed something and dare ask them for anything. Kathy wondered why they had bothered to have children.

Kathy had taken on a protective parental role toward Jake since they were children. She was five years older than him and had sworn to protect him from as much as she could. She also swore she'd provide for him as best as she could. Even though her parents both made six figures a year, neither felt Kathy or her brother were worthy of the finer things in life, or the basic necessities most times.

Kathy's grandmother used to say, "In the end, your friends are always going to let you down. It's only your family you can depend on." Kathy laughed at the memory. As a child, at least for a short time, she used to believe those words. The day her grandmother died, the realization hit that it was a farce, a cover up. The truth of her youth was that it was much less hurtful to believe they were right to try to destroy you than to accept that they didn't value you. Kathy had finally accepted that her family didn't value her, or her brother. She vowed to discontinue that particular legacy.  Kathy often told Jake that they were Ground Zero of their family tree.  Basically, since they had no one, they would start fresh, and ensure future generations of Carraways were loved and cared for.

Kathy glanced at her watch.  She had a little less than an hour to make it from the Southern Methodist campus where she had met Jake for lunch to her appointment with Judge DeShazzo downtown.  She hurried to her car so she could head that way.  She certainly didn't want to be late.  A friend of a friend had secured an interview for Kathy in the Probate Court.  If they liked her, she'd start off as an assistant to the investigator.  Eventually, she'd work as an investigator.  Though it wasn't a pilot's job, the gig paid well and provided a generous benefits package, something she desperately needed right now.

Though they had grown up in nearby Fort Worth, Kathy and Jake now rented a small house in North Dallas.  It wasn't the most fancy of abodes, but it wasn't the shabbiest either. It was in a nice neighborhood, with great schools, great neighbors, and amazing amenities, exactly as the realtor had pointed out. It was a neighborhood filled with young professionals, who burst at the seams with ambition, just as Kathy did. She had promised Jake when he graduated high school that a better life was ahead. All they had to do was not look back. With that, and Jake's scholarship to Southern Methodist University, they had fled twenty-six miles east to Dallas.

Kathy was a Horned Frog. She had attended Texas Christian University in Fort Worth on a full academic scholarship. She had dreamed of Jake being an alumnus as well, however, TCU didn't present as lucrative of a scholarship package as SMU did. Aside from that, by the time Jake finished high school, he and Kathy were both ready to abandon their troubling existence and start down a meaningful path, free from disappointment and pain.  Dallas seemed like just what they needed.

Kathy had initially worked as a payroll clerk for the Dallas Police Department after college.  Budget constraints imposed by the city manager at the time caused Kathy and 32 others to be laid off, permanently. From there, Kathy had taken two different part time jobs in order to equal the income of one full time job. She soon realized, however, that working as a bookkeeper was much different than simply keying in payroll data, and she didn't enjoy it even one little bit. She also realized fast food wasn't her forte either.

Fortunately for her, Bubba, the night manager at the Chicken Shack where she worked on Tuesdays, Fridays and Sundays had a cousin who was friends with Jenna DeShazzo, who was the niece of the probate court judge Nikki DeShazzo.  Somehow, Bubba had heard Judge DeShazzo was looking for some help and had finagled an interview for Kathy. She was unquestionably grateful.

Kathy glanced at her watch as she parked. She was twenty minutes early, which was perfect. She always got a bit antsy if she didn't arrive for appointments at least fifteen minutes ahead of schedule. Her friend Denise often joked that this was clear evidence Kathy should indeed have pursued a career in the military.

Kathy glanced in her rear view mirror. She'd brushed her hair back into a tight bun. She wanted to look feminine, but professional. According to Southwestern Professional Magazine, wearing your hair in a bun achieved this effect. Kathy smoothed the sides of her head, looking for out of place hairs, but there were none. She wore just a hint of a neutral lipstick. Her long legs, dark hair and green eyes, just like her brother's, gave her look an additional touch of intrigue and class. She had her resume in a leather attaché she had purchased for herself as a college graduation present. The navy suit she wore, another graduation present, screamed "CEO". She was ready to face Judge DeShazzo.

As Kathy entered the Dallas County Courthouse, she was impressed. The artisan work along the outside was quite intricate in detail. Inside was no different. The mahogany handrails which lined the marble staircases were well cared for and clearly of another era. Kathy stood a little taller and walked a bit straighter as she made her way to the fifth floor.

The entire floor was dedicated to matters of probate. To her left, as she exited the elevator, Kathy saw several offices marked "Investigator". To her right, she saw a door marked "Judge J. Avery", and another marked "Judge N. DeShazzo". Beside the door marked for her potential new employer, there was another smaller door marked "Clerk of the Court". Kathy slowly entered the smaller door.

A not too friendly looking, mousy woman in her mid-fifties introduced herself as Jan. She gruffly told Kathy to have a seat. Kathy picked a chair near the window. She wasn't sure how long she would have to wait, and she preferred to have a view as she sat. The skyline was blocked by some of the taller buildings, but Dealey Plaza, where President Kennedy had lost his life, was clearly visible. Kathy felt a little tug of awe at her emotions because she was so close to such history.

By the time Judge DeShazzo beckoned Kathy in to her chambers, Kathy was sweating like an old, out of shape workhorse. The air conditioner, Jan apologized, was being repaired at the moment and probably wouldn't be functional until later in the day or the following morning. Kathy wiped her brow with a handkerchief she had in her purse and followed the judge into her chambers.

The first thing Kathy noticed was the white carpet. She hated white carpeting. It always reminded her of the carpet in her home when she was a child. For just a moment, Kathy's memory whisked her back in time to a day her mother had bashed her repeatedly in the head with a glass ketchup bottle for not taking out the trash. There was so much red. It was never clear if there was more blood than ketchup or vice versa. What Kathy remembered most was how long it took to clean that darn carpet and return it to a pristine state. She doubted she would ever like white carpeting…

The next thing Kathy took in was the stunning mahogany furniture, covered in rich magenta and ivory fabric. There were several potted plants and lace doilies as accents. A grandiose bookcase rose from the floor all the way up to the ceiling. The leather bound books that lined the shelves had titles etched in gold and regally stood at attention. Classical music played softly somewhere in the rear of the office, which was approximately six hundred square feet, as far as Kathy could estimate. The scents of vanilla and freshly brewed hazelnut coffee filled the room.

Adjacent to the door, an ivory colored Queen Anne sofa sat next to a large window. Judge DeShazzo beckoned Kathy to have a seat there, next to her. Kathy didn't want coffee, but Judge DeShazzo did. She actually required it, she joked. This helped break the ice and Kathy could feel the anxiety exit her body. She relaxed even more as Judge DeShazzo made small talk.

They had both attended Texas Christian University. Judge DeShazzo had gone on to law school at Southern Methodist, the same school Kathy was praying Jake would attend for law school since he was already there for his undergrad work. They talked about this for a few minutes. Judge DeShazzo said she would be glad to help him study for his LSAT exam if he needed some help.  Kathy would definitely take the judge up on the offer, she thought silently to herself.

As they went through all the standard questions, Judge DeShazzo abruptly stopped.  She looked Kathy directly in the eyes and told her she was hired, and she'd start tomorrow.  Forget all the pretentious questioning. Something in the judge's gut told her Kathy was the perfect candidate.  Judge DeShazzo took pride in her ability to discern an individual's character.  This was an invaluable trait on the bench.

Kathy gleefully accepted the offer.  She couldn't have been more excited if she had won the lottery.  In fact, it felt like she had won the lottery.  No more working two and three part-time jobs to piece together one full time salary!  No more worries about how she would help Jake get through law school.  No more worries about anything!

Well, she thought there would be no more worries. As she left the interview and headed home, Kathy's car refused to start. It kind of coughed and sputtered like it wanted to start, but just didn't have the energy to do so. Kathy tried to start it a few more times, and finally it started. Then as she pulled out of the parking lot, she heard what sounded like her engine block exploding.

Forced to pull over to the side of the road, Kathy popped the hood of her car. She immediately managed to get a huge stain on her suit, the only real one she owned. As she fumbled to secure the hood of her vehicle in the upright position, she stepped in a crack and snapped one of her brand new heels. She looked around for help, but everyone was oblivious. Heads and eyes were glued to cell phones and other mobile devices, clueless to Kathy's dilemma.

She didn't have a cell phone anymore. She had given it up in favor of being able to afford groceries on a more regular basis. There probably hadn't been a payphone anywhere around for ten years or more. Kathy began to become distraught, when she saw a man make a beeline for her car. He looked friendly, and like he wanted to help.

Sure enough, that's exactly what he wanted to do—help. After a few cursory looks and pokes under the hood, he proclaimed Kathy's car useless.

"The engine's blown," he told her.

Kathy didn't know what that meant, but she knew it was bad. The strange man quickly picked up on the fact that Kathy knew nothing about cars and even less about engines.

"You have to keep oil in them, or they fall apart. Judging by the lack of moisture on the dipstick in the oil reservoir, I think it's been a while since you put any in there."

He then pulled out the dipstick and showed Kathy what he was talking about. She immediately reflected to the light that had been on for more than a week. It had alerted her that she needed oil, but she thought she could make it until payday next week. The rent and utilities had been due this pay period…

Kathy wondered aloud how much this would cost to repair. The mystery gentleman explained that it would be three or four thousand dollars, at a minimum. She'd be much better off to invest in a new car.

Kathy's heart sank. If she couldn't afford a quart of oil, how could she possibly afford a new car note? Or a better question was how could she even afford the down payment? The man seemed to read Kathy's mind. He reached out a slender hand to shake hers.

"I'm Rick Liriano. I own Liriano's Dodge. I can get you into a new car or truck, with no money down- regardless of your credit. Well, that is if you have a job and enough income to pay the note. Here's my card.  Give me a call today or tomorrow and I'll get one of my salesmen to put you in something nice.  I can even have this one towed to our place if you want to use it as a trade.  It won't bring you much, but at least the worry will be off your shoulders about what to do with it."

Kathy accepted the card from his outstretched hand and promised to call later that day.  She also accepted the offer to have the car towed.

She gathered her things from the vehicle as Mr. Liriano called the tow truck.  He let her know it would be there in a half hour.  He further explained that the driver would give her a ride to his car lot if she desired. He'd offer to take her himself, but he had to run to an appointment, he explained.  Kathy was grateful for this assistance.  She didn't have money for a cab and certainly had no idea how to use the city's mass transit system. She wasn't even sure a bus ran in the area.

Once the tow truck driver arrived, he made Kathy feel at ease. He was clearly knowledgeable, and his grandfatherly demeanor had a calming effect on Kathy's anxious state of mind. On the ride to the car lot, the two chatted about various things. He had been an SMU alumnus, had a distinguished career in the military from which he retired, and then took over the tow truck business from his brother who was succumbing quickly to cancer. He didn't really enjoy the "tow" part of the business, but he did enjoy helping people in distress. It was at times like this he felt he was doing God's work, and it made him feel good. He wished her well when they got to her destination and told her to let the salesman know he was in the rear with her auto.

Kathy walked over to the receptionist and asked for Rick Liriano. The receptionist had been waiting for her. She flashed a brilliant smile and pulled out a thin file folder. She introduced herself as Molly, stood up, and directed Kathy to follow her to a salesman in a small office in the rear of the showroom.

"This is Rayster Morris. He's going to help you out. Mr. Liriano already left us with specific instructions to do so."

Kathy was impressed. It was the first time in her life that she could remember anyone doing anything nice for her unprovoked. Well, except for Jake. He was always kind to her.

Rayster waved to a seat in front of his desk, and Kathy quickly occupied it. He had what appeared to be a candy buffet to the left of his desk, and told Kathy to help herself. Sodas were in the refrigerator if she wanted one. She didn't, she said. She just wanted to know what they had that was in her price range, that wouldn't require a down payment or a huge loan with unmanageable payments.

Rayster handed Kathy an application. He directed her to fill it out, telling her he could provide more information once he ran her credit report. Kathy quickly filled in the blank spaces. There wasn't much to share. Other than her house, and a credit card reserved strictly for emergencies, she'd never made payments or bought anything on credit. She'd always done it the old fashioned way—saved up until she had enough for the purchase. She glanced over the form one quick time before she gave it back to Rayster.

Rayster told her everything looked great, except one thing. She must have made a mistake on her employment. She had put this year's date under the information for The Dallas County Probate Court. He pushed the paperwork across the desk, telling Kathy to scratch through the date with one line, initial, and change the year to the correct year. Not only did her income have to be a certain amount, but also she had to have been making it for at least a six-month period. Though she had listed two other sources of income, one was extremely part time and the other had hired her less than two months ago. Plus, it seemed she had quit them both effective today, judging from the listed end dates.

Kathy suddenly heard herself explain that she had only today been hired at the court. So the date, today's date, was in fact accurate. The salesman squinted his brow. He chewed the tip of his pen for just a moment before telling Kathy "Just change it. They'll never know the difference. Mr. Liriano wants you approved, so I doubt they are really checking your references. Probably just your credit. The car comes with a GPS system. If you don't pay, we pick it up."

Kathy thought about this for a moment. Her gut screamed that it was wrong, but she was in a desperate situation. If she didn't get the car, she'd miss her first day at work and probably be fired. She always preached that if you have nothing in life, you always have your integrity. This action seemed to go completely contrary to that position.

Her foot began to tap the floor. He knees began to tremble and blood rushed to her head. Kathy thought for a moment more. She chewed vigorously on a finger nail. Finally, she made the decision to go ahead and change the date on the paperwork.

A brilliant smile flashed across the salesman's face. He took the paperwork and typed some information into the computer. It would be just a few minutes, he told Kathy, until he knew exactly what type of vehicle they could qualify her for. And sure enough, in just a few minutes, he had an answer. He could show her just about anything on the lot.

The first vehicle they looked at was a Dodge Dart. It was too small for Kathy's liking. Next they looked at a Durango. Then a Charger. Then a Challenger. Finally a Viper. Kathy narrowed it down to the Challenger and the Viper. Twenty minutes passed. She test-drove the Viper one more time. She finally decided on the Viper. According to Rayster, the monthly car payments were only be about $8 more than the Challenger.

She absolutely loved it!  It was the first new car she had ever owned.   Her last car had been manufactured the year she was born. This beautiful Viper was the first new car she had ever driven, for that matter.  And it was amazing!  Sleek, pristine and all hers!  Well, all hers and Jakes.  They were a team and big purchases were always community property in their eyes…at least until they both had their careers set and made the salaries they dreamed about.  She couldn't wait to meet Jake for dinner and take him for a drive.

When she pulled into the driveway, Jake was outside.  He chatted with a friend.  Once he realized the car was theirs, his quizzical look turned to one of glee.  Kathy exited the car so he could sit behind the wheel.  She suggested he take her for a drive.  Jake nodded in agreeance to the idea.  As Kathy hopped in to the passenger seat, she noticed Jake's eyes were closed and his head was bowed.

She had no idea he silently reminisced of the time their father had gotten a new Chevrolet convertible of some variety he couldn't remember. All Jake could recall was that it was blue. He had been playing outside when their father had told them it was time to go to the store. An excited Jake ran over and climbed into the front seat. Jake's dirty shoe had scraped across the seat as he had gotten in. The dirt left a fine dust on the white seat about the size of a quarter. A five-year old Jake had been violently snatched from the car, brought into the house and beaten with an extension cord. He had school pictures two days later. A mark in the shape of the folded extension cord was quite visible on his hand in the photo. Amazingly, no one had the gumption to inform the authorities like they do nowadays. Jake believed their mother still had the photo displayed somewhere…

Jake opened his eyes.  He smiled at his sister. He loved her dearly.  There would never be enough words to express that to her.  Rather than a quick jaunt around the neighborhood, the pair wound up at White Rock Lake.  The park was only open until sundown, so they simply enjoyed the sunset.  Sunsets always brought comfort to them both.  It was a sign that a brand new day would soon come.

## CHAPTER TWO

The next morning as Kathy got dressed for work, she had a smile that wouldn't quit. She was filled with anticipation and excitement about her new job, despite the unpleasant little headache she had. She and Jake had stopped to pick up a bottle of Champagne on their way home the night before. Jake thought it an appropriate way to end a pretty good night. They had a good laugh about the look on the store clerk's face when they paid for the purchase in quarters. It was all they had. Besides, money was money, right? Kathy laid odds that the owner of the store didn't get bent out of shape about the change the way the clerk did.

Before she headed out, Kathy called in to let Bubba know the Chicken Shack would have to find someone to replace her. She had no plans to ever go back—except possibly for the Saturday dinner special: a full rotisserie chicken, two large sides and two drinks for five dollars. Bubba could afford the insanely low price because he made his real money on Saturdays from the Veterans and little old ladies that filled the banquet room and played BINGO into the latest hours of the night. The dinner special lured them in and away from his competitor's over at Minison's Bingo Hall, which was only open on weekends and had a mediocre snack bar with no grill. The Veterans, in particular, preferred to play with a hearty meal in their stomachs. It was funny how something like a chicken could make people spend their money freely.

Kathy informed Allister the previous night that she would not be back to keep his books. She felt guilty for not giving him two-weeks' notice. He had told her not to worry. It was actually a bit of a relief to him that she was leaving to do something she'd enjoy. He confessed he was always worried about an IRS audit because it was clear that though Kathy needed her weekly paycheck, she had hated working as his bookkeeper. Kathy conceded that this was true, and the pair parted ways on friendly terms. They wished each other well and promised to stay in touch. Kathy knew it was a lie, but she participated in the ruse anyway.

As she pulled into her parking space at the courthouse, Kathy realized that despite the Motrin she had taken, her friend Mr. Headache continued to hang on for dear life. No matter. She was excited for the journey she was about to begin, and certainly would not allow a minor discomfort to stop her. She wore a black skirt with a floral print shirt and black jacket. Since she'd ruined her only pair of decent heels when her car had broken down, she wore a pair of flat black shoes from a Thrift Store. She was ready for business, and she prayed her outfit declared it.

The still not too friendly looking, mousy woman Kathy had met at her interview greeted her when she entered the office. The nameplate on the desk identified her as Jan Bates. It turned out, this woman was the Investigator. When Kathy interviewed, Jan had only filled in for a clerk who had not yet been hired. Due to budget constraints, there might never be authorization to fill the position. "Mission essential personnel only" came the mandate. Kathy was all too familiar with that. She inwardly smiled to know that the County had apparently deemed her position mission essential. In the past, she'd only held jobs in which it was quite clear she was easily dispensable.

Jan showed Kathy to her office. Kathy was delighted to have her own office. She looked around and surveyed the room. File folders were stacked upon the desk, several feet high. The IN and OUT boxes overflowed. Even the trashcan seemed to throw up its contents.

The room had newly installed carpet, and an ornate mahogany desk. In the corner stood a brass coat tree. On the adjacent wall, there was an oil painting of Lady Justice and her infamous scales. The walls had fresh paint, as evidenced by both the smell and the nearly empty can of Peach paint sitting in the corner. There were two doors in the room. One door was for access to and from the hall corridor. The other door connected Kathy's office to Jan's.

"I'm not even sure that door opens. A previous assistant misplaced the key, and we've never bothered to get another one made."

Kathy smiled. Her eyes traveled to just above the door. There was a brass clock, with large Roman Numerals. Kathy thought to herself that she would never miss a deadline with that hanging over the door.

In popped Judge DeShazzo. She was pleased to see that Kathy was twenty minutes early. She smiled broadly, and asked Kathy and Jan if they'd like coffee. Kathy did not, but Jan certainly did. The Hazelnut aroma tempted her too much to resist!

"I think I'll just sit here and sort through the files and paperwork. Maybe I'll join you tomorrow," Kathy said.

"Tomorrow?" Jan laughed. "You have no idea how much coffee we drink around here. Maybe you can join us for our second cup a little later."

As Jan shut the door behind them, Kathy realized her headache had intensified. It was all she could do to stand upright. She slid gingerly into her chair. Before she realized it, she had eased into a prone position on the floor beside her desk. Though it didn't eliminate the headache, it made it more bearable.

Kathy glanced at the clock above the door. She figured she had fifteen to twenty minutes before Jan or Judge DeShazzo came looking for her. She closed her eyes and vowed to nap for only twelve minutes…just enough to take the edge off of her headache.

When she woke up twenty-five minutes later, Kathy was momentarily panicked. She blinked and tried to get her eyes to focus. She glanced at the clock and saw the time. She also saw that the door was still closed, meaning no one had come to look for her. As she stood up, she leaned hard on the desk for support. She felt nauseous and her headache seemed to have renewed vigor. If she could just push herself through the day, she'd rest when she got home.

Just as she positioned herself in her chair and began to peek at a few files, the door opened. It was Judge DeShazzo with a can of sparkling cranberry juice for her.

"It seems you aren't a big coffee drinker, so I brought you this," she said.

Kathy accepted it from her outstretched hand. She hoped the carbonation would settle her stomach and quiet her headache.

"Thanks so much. I was really thirsty," Kathy said, with just a wee bit of distraction in her voice.

Judge DeShazzo erroneously sensed Kathy was engrossed in the files.  She called Jan in. The two pulled up chairs and faced Kathy on the opposite side of the desk.  Each file stirred emotions as anecdotes were told of families consumed in grief who tried to cope in a world without their loved ones.

One woman was destitute and now lived in a car because her husband died without a will.  He had removed her name from all of the bank accounts years ago because she was prone to gamble away every cent. She was the smoker.  She was the hell raiser.  In his mind, Mrs. Puckett would certainly be the one to die first, and he thought he'd simply take care of everything for her until that happened.  It never occurred to him to buy a life insurance policy on himself.  He had one on his wife, though.

A heart attack while he worked in his garden took Mr. Puckett first.  With no income, there was no way for Mrs. Puckett to pay the rent or much else.

Grief stricken, she had not opened the estate for probate until two months after her husband died.

By that time, the landlord of the couple's rented home was out of patience and wanted only hard, cold cash—not crocodile tears. She was evicted and no one in the world seemed to care, especially the couple's adult son who lived in New Hampshire and hadn't bothered to attend his father's funeral. Judge DeShazzo tried to hurry things along with the matters of probate, but, well, there was a process that just couldn't be sped up.

Jan had referred Mrs. Puckett to a social worker, who suggested the woman seek employment. At sixty-one, this did not appeal to her. So, she now lived in her car and ate meals at a local soup kitchen. Judge DeShazzo hoped to have her case closed in the next three weeks. The Court, meaning Kathy, would just need to do an investigation into whether or not there were more heirs. If there were none, a

Declaration of Executor status could be issued and Mrs. Puckett would have access to over $213,000 from the bank accounts, an IRA and two CDs.

Then there was the Jansen case. It seemed Mrs. Jansen had died and not told hubby number three that she had two ungrateful children that she hadn't heard from in thirty-nine years. She also neglected to inform him that they would fight him tooth and nail at the prospect of any inherited sum. They wanted him out of the "their" house. He wanted them to drop dead.

Corbin Johns had been a mild mannered, almost invisible volunteer at the local community center. He'd worked as a janitor for over fifty years. When he retired, no one suspected he had a dime. He left everything he had to a charity in Iowa. Seven hundred and sixty-two thousand dollars of his bequest was in cash, and about two million dollars in property.

Corbin's last will and testament was very clear and didn't need to go through probate.

"Then a niece materialized. She claimed they were incredibly close and she visited often, though there was no proof of this. She was willing to swear on a stack of Bibles that the very morning old Corbin passed away he had called her and told her he wanted her to have everything when he died," Jan conveyed.

"It was hardly a likely story, but the court must investigate," chimed in Judge DeShazzo.

The next file was Mrs. Mangussen. She had cut her kids out of her will a week before she died. They now disputed everything in court. Same story with Mr. Danvue. Mrs. Hettier's estate was uncontested and due to be settled in court next week. A copy of Jan's investigative report was already in the file. Same with the Washington, Portillo and Nichols cases. But the Haller case would require some extensive investigation...

Kathy's head swam faster and faster with every story.  She suddenly felt the urge to throw up.  She maintained her composure and told the ladies she needed to use the bathroom.  She'd be right back.  Both Jan and the Judge took the hint and excused themselves to their own piles of work. Jan promised to check in with Kathy at lunchtime.  She planned to eat at Shapiro's, a swanky new eatery a block away.  Perhaps Kathy would join her?

"I'd love to."

With that, Kathy scurried down the hall.

CHAPTER THREE

The next morning, Kathy felt more miserable than she ever had in her entire life. Her headache had morphed into something of a neck and face ache, too. Her movements were slow and jerky. She began to doubt it was the champagne that made her sick. She was frightened to know what the culprit was, but she knew she needed to see a doctor soon. First, though, she had to make it through the day at work. Thank goodness she'd been hired to start on a Thursday, and it was already Friday.

Jake made breakfast for her before he left for school. The note on the table said he hoped she felt better and had a great day. Kathy smiled at the thought of what a sweet kid he was as she folded the note and placed it on the table beside her plate. Jake had prepared a bowl of strawberries and granola topped with a bit of yogurt and an avocado omelet, which was one of Kathy's favorites. Her appetite had abandoned her, though.  She scraped both dishes into the dog's bowl and watched as he ravenously sucked it all in. Apparently, he liked avocado omelets, too.

She and Jake had found the dog along North Stemmons Freeway, as they departed an event at the Hilton Anatole Hotel.  He wandered about, lost.  He seemed in search of human comfort, someone to be kind to him and assure him everything was going to be all right.  Just like them.  Jake called him Ralph.  Kathy called him Jack.

No matter what he was called, the dog had been a fine protector and member of their little family for nearly three years now.  He finished his lavish breakfast and gave Kathy a soft nuzzle against her ankle.  This was how Ralph/Jack showed affection. Even he could see that something wasn't right with his human today.  Kathy bent down and rubbed him behind his ears before she headed out the door for work.

Traffic was horrendous, and she was delayed by fifteen minutes. She wasn't late, but she would have preferred to arrive early. First impressions and all. By the time Kathy entered her office, Jan and Judge DeShazzo were already in court. She had no way of knowing about the phone call Her Honor had received only twenty minutes earlier.

Apparently, Liriano Dodge's Credit Department actually did the job for which they were paid. They had called to verify Kathy's employment references. At 7:39 in the morning, no one was in the Court House to answer the phone except Judge DeShazzo. She eagerly confirmed that Kathy had just been hired to start the previous day. She listened intently as the person on the other end of the phone told her the application listed a start date from two years prior.

Judge DeShazzo did not like deception and lies. She was furious. She loathed dishonesty in any amount, and vowed to crush anyone who dabbled even the slightest bit in fabricated tales. Kathy was now in her cross hairs. She politely informed the caller that Kathy's employment hadn't worked out and she had been terminated after her first day.

It was lunch time before Judge DeShazzo made it back to her chambers. She promptly called for Kathy to join her. Instead of being asked to take a seat, Kathy was left to stand in front of Judge DeShazzo's desk, reminiscent of a teenager sent to visit the principal.

Jan stood in the corner, with her eyes to the floor, and a serious look upon her face. Judge DeShazzo wasted no time, and minced no words.

"I cannot, will not, have a liar working in my midst. Matters of probate necessitate workers of only the most upstanding moral and ethical character. Lies and liars cannot be trusted or tolerated. Not even small ones. It would degrade the integrity of the entire court and certainly lead to a scandal down the road."

The Judge then briefly recapped her earlier telephone conversation with Liriano Dodge before ordering Kathy to clear her office of any personal effects. Judge DeShazzo instructed Kathy to leave the courthouse immediately.

"Jan will collect your badge and key, and then walk you to the street to be discarded like the lying trash you are. Good luck to you, and may you learn from this to never betray another person with your tongue or actions as long as you live."

Kathy opened her mouth to defend herself, but then thought better of it. What was there to explain? She had, in fact, lied. She knew it was wrong in her gut when she did it. If she'd only followed her conscience and not listened to Rayster The Salesman who only cared about his commission from the sale, and not the integrity of the deal. How would she pay for the car now?

Jan never said a word as she escorted Kathy out of the building. She had watched intently as Kathy gathered her purse and sweater, but she never uttered a word. As Kathy exited the courthouse, she turned to tell Jan goodbye. Jan was already headed back upstairs, and never looked Kathy's way. At that moment, Kathy truly did feel like trash.

She slowly made her way to the employee lot. She walked in circles for several minutes, but couldn't find her car. She was certain she had parked in spot thirty-two, which was now occupied by a red mini-van.

She walked to a nearby coffee shop. The cashier let her use the phone to report the apparent theft to the police department. What a lousy day! Thankfully, the police were on their way to take her report.

When they arrived, there was the standard barrage of questions. The officers gathered her contact information and assured Kathy they'd do all they could to find her car.  As they were about to leave, one of the officers turned to her.

"Does the car have a GPS system?"

If so, he reasoned aloud, the dealership could remotely activate it and locate the car.  Remembering that she'd said she had no cell phone, the officer offered his so Kathy could call the dealership.  They all agreed, GPS activation would save a lot of time.

For the first time in hours, Kathy smiled.  The car did have a GPS, so she was sure they'd have no problem finding it.  Then she called Liriano Dodge.  Mr. Rick Liriano personally took her call.  He informed her that since she had applied for credit using false information, his dealership had repossessed the car earlier that morning.  Given the fact that she had lied on her application, he wouldn't be able to do business with her.  He wished her luck in finding a new vehicle, then hung up the phone.

A single tear crawled down Kathy's cheek. Before she could say anything, the officer already knew what happened. He patted her on the shoulder like she imagined a concerned father would.

"Should I still file this report?"

Kathy somberly shook her head no, as she looked at the ground. "It's been repossessed." As she looked up, one of the officers was already seated again in the patrol car. The other was still there. He continued to pat Kathy's shoulder with a look of concern.

"I have a daughter your age. I know it's tough sometimes. Why don't you call your folks and let them know what's going on? Surely they'd come pick you up."

Kathy burst into full-fledged tears.

"Surely they would not," she told the officer.

A look of sadness was upon his face. He simply couldn't imagine his daughter not being able to call him to pick her up if she were stranded somewhere.

"We'll give you a lift. Where do you need to go?"

"I live just off of Forest Lane in North Dallas. I'd really appreciate it."

"No worries. Come on."

As they approached the car, Officer Sour Face in the passenger seat rolled his eyes and shook his head as if to say, "I can't believe you're being a bleeding heart again." He remained silent, though. One mile. Two miles. Five. Six. Ten. Complete silence. Not even the police dispatcher interrupted the noiseless ride.

Finally, they reached Kathy's house. The driver opened the door for her. Officer Sour Face sat transfixed on a game on his cell phone. Kathy squinted just a bit so she could see the name tag of the officer who had shown her a bit of humanity. Officer Keough. She thanked him, shook his hand, and fiercely resisted the urge to have an emotional melt down. Kathy was on the verge of tears, and Officer Keough sensed it. He reached out to shake Kathy's hand and bid her well.

"Take care. I know it seems like the end of the world, but it's not. You'll be just fine."

Kathy nodded her head north and south in acknowledgement. She didn't know how, but she knew things would in fact be all right. She'd had to make them so her entire life, and this time would be no different.

# CHAPTER FOUR

It had been nearly two weeks, and Kathy still hadn't found work.  Reluctantly, she called Allister.  Between the Chicken Shack job and keeping Allister's financials, Allister paid the most, so she decided to call and beg for her job back.

"You want WHAT?" Allister shrieked.

He became dizzy at the prospect of Kathy's return.

"No, no and Noooooooooo.  Look, nothing personal, but you and I both know you did a lousy job because you hated dealing with numbers so much.  Why don't you call Bubba?  They always loved you over at The Chicken Shack.  I'll keep my ears open, too.  If I hear anything I'll let you know, but no, you absolutely may not come back here.  Best of luck to you, though."

With that, Allister disconnected the call.

Kathy didn't want to call Bubba.  The thought of her clothes smelling like fried foods every night tied her stomach in knots. The thought of not being able to pay bills made her stomach knot up worse, though, so she decided to go ahead and call.

"I'd love to help, but I already hired a girl to take your place. I'm sorry. You can always come down here and have dinner on the house til you find some kind of work. Your brother is welcome, too."

Kathy knew Bubba was being sincere, but a free chicken dinner just didn't seem like the answer to her problems. She was grateful, nonetheless.

"Thanks, Bubba. I really appreciate the offer, but I have to make some money, and soon. Please let me know if you hear of anyone that is hiring."

Bubba thought on this for a moment. His cousin was an Army recruiter. Perhaps he could help. Kathy had never run from a challenge, and if memory served him correctly, at one time she had considered joining the Army.

"My cousin Roy is a recruiter for the Army. Maybe he can help you out. I know he's always looking for good people. He even mentioned something about them offering enlistment bonuses of twenty thousand dollars. He's not here locally, but he can tell you what to do to get the ball rolling. Do you want his number?"

Kathy considered this option. She had long ago put her dream of military service on hold in favor of taking care of her brother. Maybe the time was finally right. Jake could manage without her for a few months while she did basic training, she supposed. Hopefully, she could get a slot right away for Officer's Candidate School. She would ask the recruiter about it when she called. She got the number from Bubba and told him she'd see him for lunch the next day. She'd tell him at that time how the talk went with the recruiter. For now, she needed to lie down. Her headache was back with a vengeance.

Kathy crawled into bed. Ralph/Jack soon followed. He whimpered for a bit of attention. Kathy gingerly rubbed behind his left ear until they both drifted to sleep.

About an hour later, unendurable pain awakened Kathy. She tried to sit up, but couldn't. The pain was too much. A strong wave of nausea overtook her. To her relief, it soon passed. She squinted and looked at the clock beside her bed. Jake would be home in just a few minutes, and she'd have him take her to the doctor. It was an expense they couldn't afford, but Kathy had begun to panic. She didn't know what was wrong with her. Whatever it was, she needed it resolved as soon as possible.

Just then, Jake walked into the house. They had a set of bells on the front door. They were typical jingle bells, of the Christmas variety. Perhaps it was a bit of paranoia that remained from their childhood, but both Kathy and Jake could breathe more easily if they knew when someone entered or left the house.  The bells tied to the doorknob offered this peace of mind.

Kathy tried to call Jake's name, but her voice was barely audible.  A few minutes later, he appeared before her, as if he knew something was wrong.  One look, and Jake knew Kathy needed to get to a doctor.

"I know you're going to say we don't have the money, but you have to get to a doctor.  I still have those savings bonds you bought for me a few years back.  They've just barely matured, but we can cash them and pay the doctor.  No arguments."  Jake's expression said he meant every bit of what he just said.

"But we don't have a car anymore.  I guess we could ride the bus," Kathy sighed.

"Well," Jake said thoughtfully, "we could always call Penny."

The suggestion caused Kathy to freeze in place. Penelope Fennimore, more commonly known as Penny, was one of Kathy's friends from high school.

Kathy and she had been very close; not quite like sisters, but definitely like cousins. The type you see a few times a year at family functions, and even though you may not have spoken all year, you instantly remember they are one of your favorite people and you can't wait to catch up and hang out.

Kathy didn't want to tell Jake, but she'd heard that Penny was strung out on some sort of drugs. That was what made her move to Dallas right after Jake and Kathy had. She was trying to change her environment. All that really changed, so Kathy had heard, was there was now a different abusive boyfriend who called the shots. Oh, and Penny had another baby since she moved to Dallas. How many did that make? Four? Kathy only knew the oldest child, Sariah. Sariah had been born about three days after her mother's high school graduation. That was the point where Kathy and Penny's lives started down divergent paths.

Kathy headed to college, while Penny headed to a minimum wage job. Kathy finished her first year of college, while Penny welcomed her second baby. And so the pattern went. The two would meet for birthday lunches and every few months speak on the phone, but that was about it. However, the truth be told, both young ladies knew the other one would forever and unequivocally be there through thick and thin.

"Before you say anything," Jake began, "I should warn you. I heard she's gotten into some drugs but I also heard she's trying to get clean. It's just a ride to the emergency room, so it's really kind of irrelevant."

Kathy smiled. Her brother was like her in so many ways: Not just his physical features, like his rich complexion, smooth skin and tall frame, but his mannerisms and demeanor, as well. Blunt and straight to the point; practical and compassionate. He was right.  It was only a ride to the hospital.  Surely Penny's reputation couldn't rub off on her.  Kathy told him to go ahead and call.

Within a half hour, Penny was helping Kathy into her twenty-year-old, extended cab pick-up truck. The truck had once been white, but now it was a shade of mulberry and had rims that glistened in the sunlight. Kathy smiled briefly to herself as she remembered the truck Penny had in high school.  From the outside, it always looked pristine and amazing.  Inside, well, not so much.  Kathy was secretly afraid a roach or ants may be hiding amongst all the trash that littered the floors. Some things never changed…

Jake wanted to tag along to make sure Kathy was all right.  She wouldn't allow it.  She wanted him to stay home and study.

"You'll be of more help to me if you stay home and start dinner.  I plan to have found my appetite by the time I get back.   Besides, it's just a headache…nothing to worry about."

Jake relented, and gave Kathy's arm a squeeze. That was their code for "I love you."  Kathy returned the gesture with a squeeze of her own.  She blew him a kiss, and hopped into the truck.  On the way to the hospital, Penny and Kathy chatted about everything in the world.  Eventually, the conversation turned to Penny's recent bout with drug usage.  She swore she wasn't an addict.  That's why she refused to call it an addiction.

"I'm really trying to get clean.  I swear I am.  I want to make sure I can breastfeed David for as long as possible.  The problem is Nick.  He keeps tempting me to sell that mess for him, because he knows I could use the money.  Lord knows I could, but if I sell, I use."

This was far more information than Kathy wanted to hear at the moment. She knew, however, that Penny, like herself, probably had no one else to talk to, so she listened patiently. Nick was Child Number 3's father. Penny would probably have stayed married to him if it hadn't been for the fact that he was in and out of the county jail constantly and wouldn't seek honest employment because he felt he could make more money as a low level drug peddler. The ironic part was that Nick had been voted "Most Likely to Succeed" when he graduated two years before Kathy and Penny. He had also been the class Salutatorian. Or was it Valedictorian? Kathy couldn't remember precisely, but she did find irony in how things had turned out for him.

The father of Child Number One had been banned from Penny and his child's life. As a courtesy for not pressing statutory rape charges, Penny's parents ordered him to "disappear." He did so quite well. Even in a world of Internet and social media, no one could find a trace of him. Penny often wondered if he was still alive.

Kurt, the father of Child Number Two, had been killed in a tragic car accident on the same day he and Penny were married. He had rented a Maserati for the wedding. One of his buddies talked him into a quick spin around the block. Kurt had been drinking at the reception, so he pitched his keys to his friend. Sadly, speed limit signs didn't matter to his friend, and Kurt wound up engulfed in flames when the car impacted into a tree as they rounded a tight corner.

Kurt's family played an active role in the child's life and made sure Penny didn't have to worry about necessities. Then, Penny met Nick. Nick didn't like Penny's "ex family," as he called them, being so close. He forbade any contact. He also kept her high and emotionally badgered. Since they didn't want for material things, Penny didn't complain. The last time Nick was put in county jail, though, Penny decided to leave. Soon after, she met her current boyfriend, Clint.

Kathy hadn't met him, but the grandmother of a mutual friend had said he was "something else." The grandmother had let on to Kathy that Clint's tall muscular frame, ice blue eyes, and wavy blond mane were like a magical potion that Penny simply could not resist. Kathy had also heard it through the proverbial grapevine that Clint was physically abusive to Penny. She wanted to ask, but right now wasn't the time. For now, she'd just listen.

Once they checked in at the hospital, it was nearly three hours before Kathy was escorted to a room in the back, so that she could wait for another forty-five minutes before she was seen. She hated emergency rooms. They smelled funny and it took entirely too long to be treated. The doctor's office was already closed by the time she decided to get treatment, though, so she would wait.

Just as she was about to drift off to sleep, Dr. Peshwar entered the room. She appeared to be about four feet tall, but she had an air about her that said she stood ten feet tall. Kathy was relieved. Perhaps this lady could actually relive her of the headache.

"What brings you here today?"

"I've had a horrible migraine for weeks. Well, actually, it's not constant. It comes and goes," Kathy explained.

Dr. Peshwar's eyes narrowed. Then she asked, "How much have you been drinking?"

"Nothing. I don't drink. Well, I had a half bottle of champagne two weeks ago, but I don't drink."

The doctor's eyes narrowed just a bit more as she asked Kathy, "Do you do recreational drugs, as well?"

Kathy did not like the doctor's tone. What exactly had she just insinuated? She verbalized this, but Dr. Peshwar didn't care. The doctor knew a filthy drunk when she saw one. Anyone could clearly see just from Kathy's manner of dress alone that she was a slovenly drunk, the doctor thought.  She became even more judgmental as she took in Kathy's mismatched socks, unkempt hair, and teeth that didn't appear brushed.  The vitriol the doctor felt became worse as she spied the woman Kathy had strolled in with.  Dr. Peshwar had treated her before.  Penelope Something or Other was her name.  If she remembered correctly, Crack Cocaine was her drug of choice.  The way these young girls carried themselves disgusted Dr. Peshwar.

"I'll order an MRI and a CT Scan just to be on the safe side, but you are drunk and no doubt suffering from a hangover.  How often do you use recreational drugs?"

Kathy was fed up with the accusations.  She clumsily jumped off the gurney.  Her intention was to give Dr. Peshwar a tongue lashing, but instead, she fainted. By the time she came to again, Kathy had been hooked up to an IV. Jake and Penelope were on either side of her bed, and held her hand.  She puzzled as to how or why Jake had arrived, but was glad to see him just the same.

Jake began to explain things for Kathy. He told her that apparently there was something called saccharomyces in champagne. Kathy had some sort of reaction to this yeast, and that's why she had the headaches. She'd be fine, Jake assured her, as he shot Dr. Peshwar a tight lipped smile. Dr. Peshwar looked at the ground. Just because Kathy had an allergy, she was not absolved from being a dope fiend, the doctor thought. She scribbled a few notes and informed everyone that she needed to go process Kathy's discharge paperwork.

A half hour passed before a nurse came in with discharge instructions and three prescriptions. All Kathy heard was "blah blah blah," but she was relieved to be headed home. Jake took her hand and helped her stand. Penny went to pull her truck around to the door so that Kathy wouldn't have to walk so far.

Kathy inched slowly down the hall and away from the Emergency Room. She stole a glance in her brother's direction. She was pretty doggone lucky, she thought, to have a brother as kind as Jake. He held her hand and made sure her gait was steady. He assured her he'd take care of her and everything would be all right.

As they neared the front door, a commotion could be heard outside. Clint had tracked them to the hospital. He seemed drunk, or high. Kathy couldn't quite tell which. She and Jake could see he was enraged about something, but couldn't make out what. She could only see his wavy blond hair blowing in the breeze.

"Let me see if I can calm him down. Wait here for a sec," Jake whispered to Kathy. Kathy squeezed his hand. Her eyes begged Jake to stay. He kissed the top of her head.

"I'll be right back.  I'm just going to calm him down before someone calls the cops."

"We can catch a cab home.  Just leave them."

"I'll be right back.  Penny doesn't deserve this. She looked out for us tonight.  I'm just going to return the favor."

Kathy watched as Jake walked out the door to talk to Clint.  She propped herself up against the information desk that was unmanned for the moment. Beads of sweat trickled from her brow.  She could see Jake stand between Penny and Clint, but she couldn't hear a word any of them said.  From the body language, she could tell a lot of shouts filled the air.  She decided to go ahead and call a cab.  It would be here in a minute and she'd take Jake home and leave Penny and Clint to finish their nonsense on their own.

Kathy scanned the desk for a phone.  There it was, covered with a newspaper.  Just as Kathy reached for the phone, a shot rang out.  Then another, and another.  Before Kathy could turn around, five shots had pierced the night air.  Hospital security ran out the door.

"Call the police!"

"There's two on the ground!"

"The shooter's still here!"

Kathy turned to face the chaos.  A flurry of people partially blocked her view.  There was no mistake about what she saw, however.  Penny lie on the ground, face up.  It was clear that she was dead. Brain matter and blood were everywhere around her. Kathy clutched her stomach.  She fought to breathe. Her shoulders curled.

A little to Penny's left, Jake was sprawled on the ground.  Kathy couldn't see around all the people, but she thought she saw his foot tremble.  She tried to scream for someone to help him, to save him, but nothing escaped her lips.  Tears choked back every sound she tried to utter. That's when Clint fired again.

The shot ripped Jake's abdomen open, and his eyes showed that he didn't feel it.  They were open wide, and said that he was already gone. Kathy made eye contact with Clint at that moment.  His blue eyes were crystalline and brittle.  There was a visible flush in his cheeks, and his right hand was clenched, yet he smirked.  He seemed pleased with the carnage he had created.  His hair flowed with the night wind as he admired his handiwork.  Then he saw Kathy.  He touched the brim of his blood-soaked Stetson, as if to acknowledge her.  He offered one final smirk before he turned and sprinted into the night.

# CHAPTER FIVE

"Your honor, he took everything from me when he committed this crime..."

Kathy, ten years wiser and now Assistant District Attorney for Dallas County, elicited this response when she asked the woman on the stand to please share with the court how her life had been changed by the perpetrator.  Kathy herself had said these same words at every appeal, and every parole hearing Clint had.  Yet in just a few hours, the man who killed her brother would be out on parole.

"Ms. Carraway!  Do you have anything further for the witness?"

"No, Your Honor.  That's all," Kathy whispered to no one in particular.

"It's been a long day.  Court is in recess until ten o'clock Monday morning," declared Judge Cox. The bang of his gavel confirmed it.

Kathy gathered her things and headed back to her office.  It was in a far more modern building across the street.  Kathy would have preferred to have an office at the actual courthouse, and not at "The County Admin Building."  She felt placement in a separate building somehow detracted from the prestige of the important work she and her colleagues did.

As Kathy approached the steps to her building, she saw a young girl who appeared downtrodden.

"Hey there!  What's the matter?  It's a bright sunny day and the weekend starts in a few hours. What more could you ask for?"

"I have to turn the money in for my school fundraiser on Monday, but I haven't sold a single candy bar."

"I'll take one," Kathy told her.  Then she paused.  "How many do you have left?"

"A hundred."

The little girl began to cry. Just then her mother walked over. Kathy smiled, and knelt down to the little girl's eye level.

"I'll take them all."

"Really?"

"Really."

"That's too kind of you. We don't have them all here with us, but I can bring them back," said the girl's mother.

"Sounds like a plan," Kathy said. "I'll be in my office for a few hours. If you want to bring them back, I'm in the District Attorney's Office, Room Seven B."

The little girl hugged Kathy around the knees. Her mother silently cried.

"This means a lot to us. Thank you. Her school is taking a field trip to the capital and I couldn't afford the fee. The only chance she had to go was if she participated in this fundraiser and sold it all. Thank you."

Kathy smiled and headed into the building. Just as she neared her office, Portia and Hanna approached. They had to be the most annoying interns to ever grace the DA's office. Thankfully, they only had about two more weeks left on their program.

"Not now ladies. I have a lot of work to do. Go enjoy your weekend."

"We just wanted to see if you needed anything before we left," Portia said in that high pitch voice that Kathy hated so much.

"No. I absolutely do not. Enjoy your weekend," Kathy snarled before she escaped into the safety of her office and closed the door behind her.

Kathy plopped her files and briefcase down on her desk, and sank into her chair. She leaned back, and closed her eyes. She focused on how hot and gummy her eyelids felt. Just then, there was a knock at the door.

"Not now.  Go away.  Enjoy your weekend," Kathy instructed grumpily.

The door flew open and in walked Robert Dawes.  Robert had been a dear friend in law school.  Like Kathy, he had similar motivation for a career in law.  His parents had been brutally murdered in a robbery, and he felt he and his brother never had a voice in the aftermath.  His life was upended, and deprivation and sordidness ruled for a while after his parents' deaths.  They never found the person responsible.  Robert dedicated his life to making sure criminals were put where they belonged, behind bars or to death.

"Robert, now is really not a good time."

"All right, but have you seen this?"

Robert tossed a newspaper in Kathy's lap.  Clint skinned and grinned on the front page in his prison garb.  Kathy examined his face closely.  He still didn't seem to show any remorse.  As she read the article, it was clear he had none. He blamed everyone except himself for what happened. He blamed the victims. He blamed his boss who had caused him stress when he fired him that day. He blamed the gun manufacturer. He blamed his dope dealer. He also blamed his doctor. That's the accusation that won him his freedom.

Clint had told his court ordered anger management counselor/psychiatrist at the time that he had thoughts that made him want to murder Penny. He even described the ways he envisioned it. His doc improperly cited doctor-patient privilege. The Appeals court declared that the doctor was no longer bound by that once Clint described in full detail his wish to kill Penny. The doc was also wrong when he prescribed Clint an antidepressant medication known to increase anger in a small percentage of patients. The Court said the doctor could have prevented Penny and Jake's slaying if he had reported all this to law enforcement.

The Appellate Court further determined that Clint had ineffective counsel, as his attorney never brought any of this up. No new trial was granted. Clint was to be released with credit for time served, and community supervision for an additional five years. What a slap in the face, Kathy thought.

"Yes, I saw it. He's due to be transported to the County Jail and processed for release in about one more hour. Yay!" Kathy said, defeat in her voice.

"I'm sorry. I wish there was a way we could block this."

Just then the phone rang. Kathy answered it on speaker phone.

"This is Kathy Carraway. How may I help you?"

"Hi, Kathy. It's Shannon. Shannon Ross. How are you doing?"

"Fine," Kathy curtly replied. She thought Shannon had called to remind her that Clint would be set free soon.

"Glad to hear that. Are you still interested in coming over here to work for me in the U S Attorney's office? I could sure use someone as sharp and passionate as you."

Kathy was stunned. Shannon had been the coolest law professor on planet earth. Everyone wanted to be in her courses. Kathy walked around like a zombie after Jake's murder, but Shannon was always able to shake her out of that. Shannon inspired Kathy to live life again.

Once Kathy passed her bar exam, she often begged Shannon to hire her. When Kathy was in law school, Shannon had been the lead prosecutor and Assistant District Attorney in the Dallas County District Attorney's Office. She specialized in drug and organized crime prosecutions. Thugs feared her, victims loved her.

Shannon left the District Attorney's Office to become the Deputy Criminal Chief over the Narcotics and Violent Crimes Section of the U S Attorney's Office. In the last year, she had been promoted. She now worked as Criminal Chief of the U S Attorney's Office for the Northern District of Texas. She supervised seventy criminal prosecutors and a support staff of fifty all across her hundred county territory. She worked closely with the FBI, DEA, CIA, The Texas Rangers and the Dallas Police Department, not to mention hundreds of others across the state and the nation.

Shannon was responsible for prosecuting a wide array of federal crimes that fell into one of the following categories: violent crimes, major crimes, organized crime, economic crimes, and special prosecutions. Shannon without a doubt had a "Don't

Mess With Texas or Jesus" attitude, so she was in the right job. Kathy had once again jokingly told Shannon outside of court a few months ago that she'd love to work for her. Shannon smiled the compliment off, and Kathy made no further mention of it.

Robert lightly nudged Kathy and prodded her to answer. Shannon had been one of his favorite professors, too.

"I'd go work for her in a heartbeat," he whispered to Kathy.

Kathy lightly ran her fingers across the keypad of the telephone. She carefully contemplated what her answer should be. She glanced at Robert, then she leaned back in her chair again, and cleared her throat.

"I'd love nothing more than to come work for you," she said with her eyes closed.

It was the truth. Right now, Kathy needed to get away from the county courthouse. With Clint getting out, it was no longer therapeutic. Rather, it was a big reminder of how the system sometimes failed. She wanted a fresh mission. She wanted something to keep her knee deep in paperwork, and too busy to think about Jake or Clint. The U S Attorney's office promised that. Besides, who didn't want to work for THE Shannon K. Ross? She was a legend in Dallas County.

"Can you start in two weeks?"

"Absolutely. I have a big case that just entered the sentencing phase. I'll be done with that by Tuesday. I can get my other cases reassigned, and I'm all yours."

"Welcome to the team. I'll see you on the twenty second. Meet me in my office at nine."

"Will do."

Just as Kathy disconnected the call, there was a knock at the door.

"Come in," Kathy directed.

In walked the little girl from earlier and her mother.  Both of them had their arms loaded up with chocolate candies.

"What's all this?" Robert chuckled.

"The perfect way to celebrate," Kathy said as she high fived the little girl.

## CHAPTER SIX

Kathy had visited Shannon a few times at work, but they'd always met in a conference room or in the snack bar. Kathy had never actually been into the suite of offices that held Shannon's unit. She was impressed. Dignity, Purpose, and The Law filled the air. Everyone here had their own office. There were no mass cubicles like there were in the District Attorney's Office.

Kathy walked toward Shannon's office. She glanced down at her new security badge and smiled. She was one of the team, she reminded herself. She stood a little straighter, and walked with a little more umph. As she neared Shannon's office, she reflected on just how far she had come since her days with Bubba and The Chicken Shack. She smiled. It had been a long road to get here, yet here she was. Her only heartache was that Jake was not here to enjoy this with her.

Just then someone tapped Kathy on the shoulder. It was Shannon. The two hugged, as was their custom.

"Well don't you look nice? It's great to have you on the team," Shannon said as she beamed at Kathy.

"I wanted to impress my new boss."

Both ladies giggled. Shannon's cell phone rang at that moment. She held her finger up, to indicate she needed just one minute to handle the call. Kathy smiled and nodded that she understood.

She wished her own phone had rung. If it had, she could have avoided the awkward pause that happened as Shannon chatted away. She looked out the window and pretended to enjoy the view. Inside, Kathy felt she'd faint. She couldn't believe that she was here in the United States Attorney's office, with an access card that proved she belonged. A slight smile crawled across her lips.  In an instant, it turned into a frown.

Jake crossed her mind again.  Kathy once more longed for him to be there to enjoy this moment with her.  Then again, this moment may not have happened if he were still around.

"Can you hear me?"  Shannon nearly whispered as she leaned into Kathy's face.  "It's ok.  First day jitters happen to us all."  She motioned for Kathy to follow her.

"Yes.  Just a little nervous.  It's not every day a girl gets to work for her law school professor," Kathy flattered as she followed Shannon.

"I'll show you to your office in just a minute.  For now, put your stuff in there.  That was Thelma on the phone.  I need to meet her in the conference room.  It might be fun for you to sit in," Shannon teased, as she pointed to her open office door.

Kathy tossed her things on the couch near Shannon's door. In the split second it took her to do so, Shannon was already halfway down the hall. Kathy nearly jogged to catch up. As she moved down the hall, she admired the artwork that donned the wall. Frieda Kahlo, Georgia O'Keefe, and even what looked like a Grandma Moses. It was an odd assortment. As she neared the end of the hallway, Kathy wondered if the personalities of her new colleagues were just as varied. She made a left turn, as Shannon had, and sped up just a bit.

This hallway faced the outside of the building, and was full of large glass windows in every direction. There was lots of sunshine. Kathy squinted. Then she saw Shannon, who waited outside the conference room door. She waved Kathy into the room.

Thelma Quince Colbert was already seated in the room. She stood when Kathy entered. Kathy froze for just a moment. She'd seen this woman in the newspaper a few times. Wasn't she from the Fort Worth U S Attorney's Office? Kathy thought she heard something about that office working on something big. Maybe this meeting had something to do with it.

"Welcome one of our newest attorneys, Kathleen Carraway. Kathleen, this is Thelma Quince Colbert. She heads the Civil Litigation unit at the Fort Worth DOJ Office," Shannon announced.

"Kathy. Please, just call me Kathy."

The two women shook hands. Thelma, almost undetected, assessed Kathy from head to toe. She looked the part. If Shannon had brought her to this unit, she must, of course, fit the bill for what they needed on this case, and in this unit: someone who could kick seemingly insurmountable odds in the face and score a win for the little guys.

The women took seats at the table. There was a smorgasbord of paperwork spread out on the table.

The whiteboard on the wall that faced them was filled with dates, names of people, alleged offenses, and one ominous name in the center:  Novation.

Kathy had no idea what Novation was, but she was certain it was horrible and dangerous.  She glanced at Shannon, who fixed an intent gaze on the paperwork on the table.  Shannon read page after page.

"We have a Whistleblower alleging Medicare fraud against Integrated Health Services," Thelma began to explain for Kathy's benefit.

"That's something DOJ gets involved in?" Kathy queried.

"Well, normally, no.  However, this case is one of the most complex, organized cases of fraud we have ever witnessed."

"The original lawsuit was filed here in Dallas last year by a social worker at the IHS facility," Shannon began.  "Basically, she simply alleged that her employer was billing Medicare for treatment that patients never received."

"Then a few things happened that lead to the original complaint being sealed until DOJ could look into things," Thelma added.

"A few things?" Kathy asked.

"Actually, more than a *few* things," Shannon said as she continued to scan the paperwork before her.

"Yes. Far more than just a few. Our interest was piqued when Mike Weiss died under mysterious conditions," Thelma went on.

"That junkie lawyer out of Houston?" Kathy asked, incredulous.

"He may have had his vices. We all do. But he was sharp as a tack. He was on to something, and we believe it may have cost him his life," Thelma shared, as she pounded the table for effect.

"I thought he died of an overdose. No?" Kathy asked, confused.

"Well, it's true that he had a lethal amount of heroin in his system when they found his body, but Shannon and I don't think he is the one that put it there," Thelma went on.

"But why would someone kill him?  Over Medicare fraud?" Kathy asked.

"It is a lot more complicated than that," Shannon inserted, though she didn't look up from the papers.

"Yes.  It's far more complicated than that.  We are looking at fraud on such a grand scale, we can't even define the damages yet.  May I?"  Thelma looked to Shannon.

Shannon gave a nod of approval as she said "I plan to have Kathy assist you on this case."

With that, Thelma began to fill Kathy in on the details of the case.  It had actually begun years before.  It was also filled with more twists and turns than any modern day soap opera.

About ten years before Kathy sat and listened to the tale in the U S Attorney's office, an inventor kicked off the chain of events that would become central to the story. He had devised a one-use syringe that would prevent nurses and other healthcare workers from getting stuck with contaminated needles.

Contaminated needles transmitted a number of diseases such as hepatitis and HIV, and many other life threatening illnesses and diseases. Those that worked in healthcare loved the devices. They begged for the devices. They were tired of contracting diseases or going through cycles of health scares after getting accidentally stuck. The National Institute of Health was so enthralled with the product that they gave the inventor a grant to develop the needle. The inventor also hoped this would end the reuse of needles around the world by drug addicts.

The syringe was fairly cost effective and clearly had many benefits. Despite this, hospitals across the country refused to allow the inventor to show the product to purchasing agents. Just like illegal street drugs were distributed and sold through cartels that profited greatly, often at the expense of others, the same was true for medical products.

Though this product was innovative, the inventor was a small fish in the game of kickbacks. There was another manufacturer of needles which was a comparative giant. This company paid millions every single year to hospitals to ensure that their product, and no others, were used. It didn't matter how unsafe the larger manufacturer's product was. The group purchasing organizations at the hospitals didn't allow any other products to be considered, if they couldn't pay the expected kickbacks. So, the inventor decided to file a lawsuit.

He retained the services of Mike Weis and Paul Danzinger in Houston. The two attorneys did their own fact checking, and were alarmed and appalled at what they found:  a pay to play system in America's healthcare industry.  Despite the myriad of safety concerns the auto-retractable single use syringes could mitigate or eliminate, if the inventor couldn't grease palms the way the big boys did, his invention would never see the light of day. They immediately filed a lawsuit.

Interestingly, there was little support for their cause.  Weiss' own Senator even attempted to discourage him from going after the healthcare industry.  In addition, there were a number of threats from the underworld.

Weiss' office had been ransacked.  He was harassed.  He was stalked.  He was followed. Clients left.  His partner, Danziger, was ready to throw in the towel.  He had a wife, and a baby on the way.  Why subject himself to such undue stress when he could focus on other cases that the firm could actually win?

Now, everyone in Houston, and probably Dallas, knew that Mike Weiss liked to party. When he had a case or needed to be alert to teach a class, though, he never partook of the street drugs he'd come to love so much. So, it seemed pretty odd when he was found by his housekeeper, apparently dead from an overdose. Even odder to Thelma and Shannon was the fact that authorities did not pursue an investigation into the thirty-two-year-old Weiss' death. Shannon had been the U S Attorney assigned to the case, and still wanted answers about Weiss' death, and justice for the inventor. She initiated a criminal investigation against the group purchasing organizations, or GPOs as they were more commonly known.

Just after Weiss died, a social worker for Integrated Health Services in Dallas became a Whistleblower. Carolyne Gray, the social worker, let DOJ know that they routinely admitted patients who did not need their level of care, and then billed Medicare for services not provided.

In one particular instance, the facility stated a patient was admitted for a fractured hip, a stroke, and a motor vehicle accident that caused chest trauma. The patient's family let DOJ know that the car accident was some twenty years ago, and the stroke more than two years ago. There was an endless supply of others with similar discrepancies.

One elderly woman was admitted for pulmonary problems. Interestingly, she never once had a pulmonary consultation. She was also well enough to leave on daily outings with her spouse. There was also the issue of specialists working together on patients, and then charging for a full hour of skilled care even though they may have spent only ten minutes with the patient.

Just as Thelma Quince Colbert had gotten the go ahead from Shannon to intervene in the

Whistleblower case, another fraud case reared its head. Samuel Lipari, from Kansas City, had recently stood up a company called Medical Supply Chain. The company was created to give hospitals a way to purchase any supplies they needed directly from the people that manufactured them. This meant hospitals could side-step GPOs such as Novation and Neoforma. It also meant health care consumers, also known as patients, could save somewhere in the neighborhood of $80 Billion every single year.

This should have been cause for celebration. Instead, it was cause for great consternation. At least that's how the GPOs reacted. Then, the "forces that be" seemed to go into attack mode on Lipari's company. This was noted when Lipari was turned down for a bank loan.

"Turned down for a bank loan? What does that have to do with the GPOs?" Kathy questioned, as she leaned in toward Thelma, both her elbows propped on the conference table.

"Well, it had a lot to do with the GPOs, as it turns out," Thelma assured her.

The bank loan had literally been approved in one moment, and taken away in the next. When Lipari went to finalize the documents, that is when he was told the bank had changed its mind and would not loan him the funds he needed for his business. When pressed as to the reason, the bank cited a provision of the USA PATRIOT Act.

"The PATRIOT Act?" Kathy asked, confused.

"Yes. The PATRIOT Act. The bank said that Lipari could not really give all correct answers on the source and flow of money as dictated by the PATRIOT Act," Shannon shared.

"Since Lipari's business was in good standing with the State of Missouri, and had clearly traceable funds…," Thelma went on, "and he was a U S citizen, it didn't add up for the bank to tell him this. Something wasn't making sense, so he decided to do his own digging to find out why the bank seemed to be in bed with the GPOs."

"As it turns out, the bank has a relationship with the investment firm Piper Jaffray. Piper Jaffray has a relationship with Novation and Neoforma," Shannon continued.

"Which bank is this? And who or what is Neoforma?" Kathy asked.

"U S Bank is our bad guy. Neoforma is another GPO," Thelma clarified.

"And it looks like the bank denied funds to Lipari because U S Bank and Novation, at the behest of Piper Jaffray, conspired to keep Lipari's business out of the marketplace?" Kathy concluded aloud.

"Bingo!" Shannon quipped.

"Has Lipari filed any sort of lawsuit?" Kathy pressed.

"He has; a civil suit a couple of years ago.  It still hasn't been heard in court yet.  However, I think Thelma may have just brought us enough information to launch a criminal investigation into the entire medical supply industry, with Novation at the center of it all," Shannon shared, as she resumed reading the mound of paperwork before her.

"Do you want to notify Counsel to the White House, or should I?" Thelma asked.

"I'll fill them in.  I'll call Alberto Gonzales.  He and his team have been in denial since we first started these investigations a year and a half ago.  I'll make them understand that there's more to it than just money laundering and Medicare fraud," Shannon announced with a hint of fury in her voice.

"Yes, indeed," Thelma agreed.

"Do you still have your contact over at the New York Times?" Shannon asked Thelma.

"Of course I do," Thelma beamed.

"Let's give them a ring. After I speak to Alberto, I want them to really feel the pressure," Shannon decided aloud.

"Consider it done," Thelma said with a smile.

"If you don't mind, leave these with me for a bit. I want to have them on hand when I talk to Alberto," Shannon said as she waved her hand across the mound of papers on the table.

"Sure. I'm going to head back to my office. I'll pick these up in a few days," Thelma said as she stood.

She gathered her briefcase and purse, then turned to Kathy, who instinctively bounced to a standing position.

"It was nice to meet you, Mrs. Colbert," Kathy relayed.

"It was a pleasure to meet you, as well. I look forward to working with you soon. And please... Call me Thelma."

## CHAPTER SEVEN

The next morning began with a press conference outside the U S Attorney's Office in Dallas County. There was a sea of microphones from what seemed like every media outlet in the country. The men and women who manned them clamored to make sure they got stories back to their networks first. They didn't realize the New York Times already had an exclusive interview with one of the U S Attorneys. They wouldn't discover this for a few more weeks. Shannon, ever the charismatic speaker, took command of the audience as she stepped to the podium and shared her brilliant smile.

"First, I want to say thank you for coming out today, and helping me spread the word. There are some slimy creatures hiding in darkness, and the United States Attorney's Office intends to shine an incredibly large and foreboding light on them," Shannon began.

She paused for effect and slowly scanned the room.  Gail Newsome from KDFW was on hand. George Motserrat from WFAA was there.  Several other favorites who Shannon recognized smiled back at her, as well.

"Based on numerous federal codes, investigators from my office are seeking evidence of healthcare fraud, conspiracy to defraud the United States, theft or bribery involving programs which receive federal funds, obstruction of investigation and other possible violations.  We are looking at multiple, massive cases of fraud and expect to file in every one of them.  In fact, we have already filed in many.  I have signed a number of subpoenas, and I am placing Novation, U S BancCorp, the investment firm Piper Jaffray, and the rest of those somehow involved in the healthcare industry on notice," Shannon declared.

"What exactly does this mean?" a reporter queried.

"You know that saying Don't Mess With Texas?"

The reporter nodded her head that she did.

"Well, don't mess with the U S Attorney's Office either," Shannon said with her signature wink.

"So, the common link in all these cases is fraud?" a reporter bellowed from the back of the crowd.

"The common link in each and every single one of these cases is Novation," Shannon declared. Once more, she paused for effect before she continued.

"Novation is a company that has its headquarters right here in North Texas. While remaining unknown to the average citizen, Novation is the largest broker of hospital and medical supplies in the entire country. They wield an enormous influence over the lives of patients, the safety of hospital workers, and the astronomical costs of healthcare in this country, that only continue to creep higher and higher," Shannon asserted.

"There are some small medical supply manufacturers that we've talked to that are painting a picture of not being allowed to compete because they can't pay to play.  Couple this with all the other things, like Medicare fraud, and you have a travesty being perpetrated upon the citizens of our dear country," Shannon said as she placed her hand over her heart.

She then did an about face and scampered away to her office.  The reporters clamored for more information.  There would be nothing further for them today.  As Shannon neared her office, she could hear the phone ring.  She moved a little faster and picked it up before it could ring again.

"This is Shannon Ross.  How may I help you?"

"Shan Non Ross," the caller declared, as he prolonged the sound of the syllables of her name.  "Why in the fuck did you just declare war on the healthcare industry?  I thought I was clear on this when we spoke yesterday evening."

"First of all, language, Alberto.  Once you start using the F word, I can't understand anything else you have to say.  Secondly, in the words of the immortal Katherine Graham, I wasn't asking your permission last night.  I was letting you know what was going to happen.  I don't tell you how to do your job, and you certainly do not tell me how to do mine."

"Let me explain to you how we do things around here…"

"No, Alberto, let me explain to *you* how *we* do things around here.  First and foremost, we do things that are legally, ethically and morally correct and just.  We believe in fact, not conjecture.  We believe in honor, integrity and personal courage.  And we don't scare off easily, even when the bullies in Washington want us to.  You have a beautiful, blessed day.  I've got work to do, so I'm going to let you go now.  Talk to you later."

Alberto Gonzales sat stunned.  He stared at his telephone receiver for just a moment before he hung it up.  Shannon had gotten under his skin, again. She was hindering his political ambitions and was probably too ignorant to even care.  Why couldn't she just do as she was told, like the others?  No one refused to do his bidding, except Shannon, and he was tired of it.

He needed a drink.  He looked at his watch.  It was barely nine AM.  Then, for just a moment, he could hear his deceased mother.  "Mijo, alcohol is for the wicked.  You're not wicked, are you?"  He wasn't sure anymore.

Many things in Alberto Gonzales' life caused him to question if he was wicked. He would ponder the question for only a fleeting moment each time, and this time was no different.  He had political ambitions, and refused to let something as mundane as a conscience derail his dreams.

That had been more than evident in the last few years as he dealt with fallout when he supported the President's policy of enhanced interrogation techniques. That is what it was called internally. Outside the White House, people referred to it as "torture of detainees."

It may have been more accurate to say Gonzales was the catalyst for the creation and implementation of the President's policy than to call him a supporter of it. In his current role as Counsel to the White House, he had drafted a memo that looked into whether or not Section III of The Geneva Convention applied to Al Qaeda and Taliban fighters. (Section III dealt with the treatment of Prisoners of War.) Though the document made arguments both for and against providing Prisoner of War protections to these two groups, the ultimate tone of the paper was that the United States should not do so.  The paper didn't say this in forthright language.

Instead, Gonzales used strong insinuations that were conveyed when he opined "the old ways may not work here."  He expounded in a section of the memo that stated The Geneva Convention provision was "outdated and ill-suited for dealing with captured Al-Qaeda and Taliban fighters:  the war against terrorism is not the traditional clash between nations adhering to the laws of war that formed the backdrop for Prisoner of War protection.  The nature of the new war places a high premium on other facts, such as the ability to quickly obtain information from captured terrorists and their sponsors in order to avoid further atrocities against American civilians, and the need to try terrorists for war crimes such as wantonly killing civilians."

The memo went on to authorize ten specific techniques the CIA and other government interrogators wanted to use. The list consisted of attention grasp, walling, facial hold, facial slap (insult slap), cramped confinement, wall standing, stress positions, sleep deprivations up to 180 hours, insects placed in a confinement area and water boarding. These techniques had previously each been illegal under the United States and International law, as well as treaties. These forms of treatment were considered not just controversial by the United Nations Convention, but inhuman and degrading forms of torture.

This memo had caused great consternation for Gonzales in the court of public opinion. The press roasted him alive every chance they got. People across America roasted him often, and unrelentingly. Fortunately, in the last few weeks, things had begun to wane. Blame had somehow been heaped almost totally upon the President.

Gonzales was a staunch supporter of the President, but he'd grown weary of so much negative attention. He also knew that the more tongues wagged about how he had authorized torture, the less likely he was to be chosen as United States Attorney General. That was the one last chess move he wanted to complete in his career before he retired to teach or lecture.

That was why this deal with that U S Attorney, Ross, gave him heartburn. If DOJ took on the entire healthcare industry, many scandals were sure to unfold. Much money and many jobs would be lost, and how could that help anyone? Many skeletons were sure to fall out of closets…including his own.

Gonzales had previously been a partner with the law firm of Vinson and Elkins LLP. Novation was one of the firm's largest clients. The public wouldn't understand. The U S Attorney's Office wouldn't understand.  It wasn't some travesty, as Shannon had told the media.  It was just business.  Business as usual.

Why couldn't Shannon Ross and Thelma Colbert just let it go?  Whatever reasons they thought they had, he vowed to make sure they stopped dead in their tracks and abandoned this asinine investigation.  No one would derail his career.  Period.

He yanked open his bottom desk drawer and looked at the bottle of Scotch.  It was an expensive brand and looked absolutely delicious at that moment.  Then he heard his mother's voice again.

"Mijo, alcohol is for the wicked.  You're not wicked, are you?"

This time he answered.  "Maybe just a little bit, mi madre.  Aren't we all?"

# CHAPTER EIGHT

Thelma drove from her office in Fort Worth to the Dallas office to meet with Shannon for the fourth time in seven days.  She wasn't sure she had ever been to the Dallas office that much in her entire tenure with DOJ.  This was a huge case, though.  Everything had to be done just right so that the harshest punishments possible could be obtained.

As she eased off of I 30 into downtown Dallas, Thelma remembered she was supposed to meet her daughter for lunch.  That would be impossible since she was now thirty miles away from their home in Fort Worth.  She touched her dash and activated her cell phone's Bluetooth.

"Call Lilly."

The phone obeyed the command it was given.  After two rings, the call was answered.

"Let me guess, Thelma.  You're not going to be able to make it for lunch, right?"

"Who are you calling 'Thelma,' Child?"

Both women broke into laughter at the question.  Ever since Lilly was a small child, whenever she wanted to let her mother know she was annoyed, she would call her by her first name.  Thelma thought she had outgrown this when she went to college.  Apparently she had not.

"Mommmmmmmm!  We didn't even get to enjoy the Fourth of July because of this case you're on.  Can we pleasssssssssse just enjoy one little meal and pretend we're the most important thing in the world to each other?"

"How can I say no to a request like that?  You are the most important thing in the world to me."

"I know.  I'm sorry.  I just…miss you.  I mean, I know we live in the same house and everything, but you're my best friend.  Medicare fraud and the healthcare industry have hijacked you.  I want you back."

"I haven't gone anywhere. I'm right here, working away so I can pay your college tuition."

"And I appreciate that a lot, Mom. I told you I can get another job and help cover things, though."

"This is your last year undergrad. I need you to focus and graduate with high marks so you can get into that medical school you keep talking about. That's your j-o-b right now. Plus, it helps me to have you available to help out around the house more. I simply do not have time right now. Speaking of that, I sincerely do not have time for lunch today. How about we have dinner instead? Maybe you can make that Hungarian dish you do, and I'll pick up a bottle of that yummy pomegranate wine we both like."

"Sounds perfect. What time do you think you'll be home? I'll have the food piping hot when you get here."

"I should be there by six thirty," Thelma said as she whipped into a parking spot next to Shannon's car.

"Ok. See you then. Love you."

"I love you, too. Lots and lots. Forever and ever."

Thelma disconnected the call. She stared at her briefcase. The information it contained was more precious than gold to her. The information she had in her briefcase held the power to revolutionize the healthcare industry and perhaps even change the course of history in many ways. She was in awe that she was a part of this. She couldn't wait to tell Shannon about the latest discrepancy she had uncovered. She scooped up her bag and headed toward the office building.

As she went through security, Fred Jones was already in line. He worked upstairs on the third floor. He was a United States Marshal, and temporarily pulled light duty after hernia surgery. He turned slightly and greeted her with the friendliest smile he could muster. It was clear that he had a little crush on Thelma. Ordinarily, she'd scowl at him. This was her best effort at saying "I'm not interested." This time, however, she glowed all over. She met his eyes and shared a striking smile.

"Good morning, Fred," Thelma said as she walked through the metal detector behind him.

Fred was shocked she had spoken to him. He was prepared to just stand there grinning like he always did when she refused to speak. Now, he was confused. He didn't know what to say. So, he just stood there and grinned from ear to ear as usual, but with a little more enthusiasm. Thelma chuckled out loud and walked around him to the elevator.

As she got off the elevator upstairs, Kathy and Shannon walked toward her.

"Great!  Glad to see you!  I was just about to call you to find out what time you were coming by," Shannon greeted Thelma.

"Well, here I am!" Thelma teased back.

"Do you have anything salacious for me?" Shannon salivated.

"Do I ever!  Come on.  Let's go to the conference room," Thelma suggested.

"I don't know what could be juicier than what you already shared," Kathy started, "but I'm dying to know!"

All three women gave a light hearted laugh, and made their way to the conference room.  Shannon took a seat at the head of the table, and Kathy sat to her left side.  Thelma chose to stand.  She was too excited to sit.  This information was surely enough to elicit an indictment and the biggest scandal ever uncovered in healthcare history.

Thelma pulled a thick packet of paperwork out of her briefcase and handed it to Shannon. She pulled another out and gave it to Kathy.

"Did you forget you already gave me copies?" Shannon asked.

"No, I didn't already give you copies. This is all new information," Thelma proudly announced.

Shannon looked from Thelma back to the paperwork, then back to Thelma. Suddenly, her game face was present. So was Kathy's. Thelma must have given them at least four-hundred pages of documentation.

"Well, start spilling the beans. I'll read it piece by piece later," Shannon prodded.

"The first thing you need to know is that it isn't just Novation. Merck, Bristol-Myers Squibb, Genentech, G E Healthcare and Cardinal Health are also big players in this game," Thelma announced.

Kathy glanced at Shannon out the corner of her eye. Shannon still had her game face on. Her fourth quarter, ten seconds left in the game, game face. Shannon leaned forward, both elbows on the table, and rubbed her hands together.

"What can we prove?" She asked.

"My team has found evidence of healthcare fraud, conspiracy to defraud the United States, theft or bribery involving programs receiving federal funds, obstruction of investigations and that's just the beginning. It's all there in the file you are holding," Thelma revealed.

Shannon took a deep breath. She slowly opened the folder and began to quickly scan the documents inside. She paused on one.

"So, we can prove that Novation members are purchasing hospital supplies through Novation, and only Novation, meaning that Novation is in fact acting as the gatekeeper with the ability to either impede or allow others to enter the hospital supply market," Shannon confirmed.

"Yes," Thelma began. "We can prove that this anti-trust violation occurs on a regular basis.  In fact, we can prove it is the norm," Thelma said.

"What else?" Shannon asked.

"We can also prove that GE Medical, which belongs to Novation, and its President Jeffrey Immelt devised a plot at the behest of General Electric's CEO Jack Welch to obstruct Internet hospital supplies by organizing the other members of Novation in an agreement to block new entrants through per se restraints of trade, including refusal to deal, market share allocation, interlocking directors, and multi-year exclusive  supply contracts procured with bribes paid to hospital administrators and a scheme to give rebates without reporting the savings to Medicare. We can also prove extortion of medical supply manufacturers, including shares in supplier corporations and kickbacks to Novation in order to be permitted to sell supplies to member hospitals and other health systems across the nation," Thelma pronounced.

Shannon took another deep breath. She had recently decided to retire from law and go into Christian ministry full time. In fact, she had just been awarded a full scholarship to Texas Christian University's Brite Divinity School in Fort Worth. She was set to begin in the fall. This case could change all of that.

One of the reasons she'd brought Kathy over was to ensure some good people would be in place when she left. The United States Attorney's Office for the Northern District of Texas served an area that encompassed roughly 96,000 square miles in northern and western Texas. Not only did they prosecute a lot of crime, but they handled the seizures/forfeitures of assets involved in these crimes.

Trustworthy, experienced attorneys, who could see beyond themselves and commit to making the world a better place were best suited for this work. Kathy fit that bill. Now, however, Shannon felt Kathy may have been a little green to take on a case of this magnitude by herself if she left. Getting whomever was chosen as Shannon's replacement spun up could delay the case by months, even years. For the sake of continuity and expediency, Shannon realized she couldn't leave just yet.

"Let me look all of this over tonight, Thelma. I'm sure it's all there, but just let me go over it before I sign the indictment," Shannon requested.

"Of course," Thelma said.

"What do you need me to do?" Kathy asked Shannon.

"First and foremost, read through everything. *Everything.* Then read it again. Memorize it. Then you know the deal. Find any and all precedents or parallel cases. I'm thinking you won't find much, but let me know what's out there. I'm going to have you as third chair on this, and you'll need to understand every detail of what's going on," Shannon informed her.

Shannon stood before she directed her attention back to Thelma.

"Thelma, I will need you here bright and early. By six A.M kind of early. I want you here as I let the boss know I've requested an indictment," Shannon said before a brief pause. "No. Scratch that. I'll get the indictment signed tonight. Be here early anyway. We have lots of prep work to do."

"Got it," Thelma sounded off.

"Ladies. Relax tonight and get some rest. Clear your minds and reenergize your spirit. We have just launched a war," Shannon said in all seriousness.

"Yes, indeed," Thelma agreed.

Shannon pulled the women into a circle. As was her custom before she undertook anything in the courtroom, she prayed with her team for God to be a part of every detail, and that His will would be done. She felt a special need to pray at this moment, though, and not wait until tomorrow when the entire team was assembled.

"Dear Father, I would ask that you help us to open our hearts, our minds, our wills and our emotions to your commandments. I pray that you help us to discern what is true from what is false. In the name of your son Jesus Christ of Nazareth, I pray that a hedge of protection be placed in front of, behind, above and below each of us this day, and every day. Father, I pray you help us stay focused on the tasks you have for us, no matter how rocky the road becomes. Help us to always remember what we already know: that you will protect us Father, and we shall not be afraid. In Jesus name, Amen," Shannon prayed.

"Amen," Thelma and Kathy declared at the same time.

"I'll see you both tomorrow, bright and early. I actually have an evening of relaxation and great food planned with my daughter, and I'm looking forward to it.  So, if there are no objections, I'm out of here," Thelma said.

"By all means," Shannon told her.  "Enjoy and tell Lilly I said hello.  Is she still at TCU?" Shannon asked.

"Yes, and this is her last year.  Well, her last year before medical school," Thelma shared.

"Wow!  Time certainly flies.  I remember when we were talking about her junior high graduation.  Now she's about to graduate college!" Shannon reflected.

"I know.  It's crazy!  Listen, I'm going to get out of here before I hit traffic," Thelma said.

"What traffic?  It's barely 3 PM," Kathy chided.

"Shhhh.  Don't tell the boss lady I'm playing a little end of day hooky!" Thelma teased in return.

Thelma nearly ran to the elevator. She hadn't been off this early in a while, and she knew that in the coming weeks she almost certainly would not. She enjoyed herself when she hung out with her daughter, so she wanted to take advantage of this opportunity.

As the elevator doors opened, Alberto Gonzales stepped off. Thelma recognized him, but what was he doing in Dallas? Wasn't his office in DC? It seemed kind of strange an advisor to the White House would pop in to the DOJ and not the other way around. Thelma greeted him.

"Good afternoon, sir."

He replied to her pleasant greeting with a sour stare and headed toward Shannon's office. As he entered the office, he surveyed the room. Kathy sat on the couch, surrounded by mounds of paperwork. Her head was buried in them. Shannon was on the phone, with her back turned toward the door. Alberto tapped Kathy's shoulder.

"You.  Out!" he barked, and pointed toward the door.  Kathy was too stunned to respond.  She recognized Gonzales from a photo that hung in the foyer.  She'd heard rumors of his sometimes nasty demeanor.  She quickly realized the rumors were true.  Shannon turned around at that moment.  Kathy looked at Shannon, unsure of what to do.

"Maura, I'll call you back," Shannon said as she locked eyes with Gonzales.

"Out!" Gonzales shouted at Kathy, as he turned away from Shannon for just a split second.

"Who do you think you are, coming into my office acting like a demon?" Shannon asked Gonzales before she addressed Kathy.  "Kathy, you stay right where you are.  It's always good to have a witness in position when you are dealing with White House Counsel."

"Excuse me?" bellowed Gonzales.

"What can I do for you, sir?" Shannon asked.

"Care to sit down? Want a cup of coffee? Maybe a tranquilizer? You seem a little uptight," Shannon observed.

"I'm uptight because you continue to lead this office astray!" Gonzales said.

"Astray?"

"Yes. Astray. I told you a year ago to quit digging and let this healthcare fetish of yours go. The DOJ cannot commit funds or manpower in pursuit of frivolous lawsuits."

"Interesting that you should storm in here today about this. I'm actually preparing an indictment in that matter."

"An indictment against whom?" Gonzales asked, almost inaudibly. He was stunned.

"Against all the leaders of that pack of wolves. Novation. Merck, Bristol-Myers Squibb, Genentech,

G E Healthcare, Cardinal Health and a whole string of others," Shannon triumphantly shared.

"What is it you think you can charge them with?" Gonzales taunted.

"Have a seat," Shannon instructed.

Gonzales took a seat on the sofa next to Kathy, who was still frozen in place. He cocked his head back, closed his eyes and massaged the bridge of his nose. Kathy wanted to move, but she was afraid she'd provoke his fury again. She decided to just stay put.

"Once upon a time, there was a group purchasing organization called Novation," Shannon began.

It took about two and a half hours to divulge every bit of information, or at least the juiciest parts. Shannon and Kathy both were convinced Gonzales would be pleased after he heard all the details. He wasn't. He remained eerily silent for exactly one minute. Then he launched into a tirade neither Shannon nor Kathy were prepared for.

Gonzales stood, leaned across Shannon's desk, and positioned himself within centimeters of her face. Their noses nearly touched. Shannon could feel the dampness of the sweat that trickled down his brow. She could almost smell his blood boil.

"The White House does not need an embarrassment from this office. You're going to forget about these fairytales you have crafted, and find real matters to pursue. Got it?" Gonzales snarled in a whisper that spat vitriol all over everyone in the room.

Kathy was stunned. Shannon was angry and had a renewed sense of purpose. She gripped the edge of her desk and silently counted to ten. She continued to look Gonzales directly in the eyes for just a moment more. He might be the Alpha in his neck of the woods, but not here in her office.

"Out!" Shannon ordered as she stood.

"What?" Gonzales asked, more confused than angry.

"Get.  Out.  Then again, if you'd like to be slapped with obstruction, I will be sure to oblige you," Shannon offered.

Gonzales looked around the room.  This wasn't over.  If Ross wanted to have a power struggle, he'd crush her.  He'd show her no mercy.  He arrogantly smirked, and took a step back from the desk.

"Good day, Miz Ross," Gonzales said as he left the office.

Kathy and Shannon could do nothing but look at each other in the seconds after he departed. Shannon finally reached into her upper left desk drawer and removed a bottle of aspirin.  She toyed with the idea of taking one or two.  She finally decided on three.

"Should I leave?" Kathy asked.

"No. Stay right where you are and keep doing what you were doing. I'll keep doing what I was doing: preparing this indictment," Shannon said as she popped the pills into her mouth and chased them with some water.

Meanwhile, in Fort Worth, Thelma and her daughter sat at their formal dining table, with a beautiful meal before them. They typically ate at the kitchen table, but when they wanted to "feel fancy," as Thelma called it, they'd make use of the intricately crafted formal table.

Lilly had set the table with the Bernardaud Eden Turquoise place settings. Thelma owned several sets of fine china and porcelain, but this pattern was her favorite. The salesman had sold her when he explained it embodied the innovative spirt common to French luxury houses. Thelma's house wasn't French, but she could dream.

"This meal was really good, hon. What do you call it again?" Thelma asked Lilly.

"Tarhonya. It's pretty easy to make. I can show you how to make it."

"Yes, please, and thanks."

"I don't mind showing you. It's no big deal. Really."

"No. I mean thank you for you being, well, you. You're such a blessing. I can't even describe how thankful I am to be your mother."

"Awwwww. Well, thanks, Mom. I totally feel the same way about you. I know it sounds cliché, but you are literally the best mom in the world. You've always been my biggest cheerleader, and because of that, I've been able to do so many things I probably couldn't or wouldn't without you. And I enjoy your company, too. I never went through one of those phases where I didn't want to hang out with you or be seen in public with you.  I've always admired you and kind of wanted to grow up and be like you."

Thelma took a sip of wine, then rose from her chair.  She walked around the table and hugged her daughter's neck.

"I love you, Lilly," Thelma whispered.

They hugged each other tightly.  Lilly asked Thelma if she wanted to watch a movie.  Thelma thought about this for just a moment.

"I *want* to watch a movie, but I have to be up a few hours before the crack of dawn.  May I have a raincheck, please?" Thelma pleaded.

"Yeah, sure.  No problem. Summer school has me loaded up with homework.  I need to study anyway."

"All right.  You do that, and I'm calling it a night.  I'll see you in the morning," Thelma said as she blew a kiss to her daughter and headed to bed.

## CHAPTER NINE

Shannon glanced at her watch. It was already six-thirty. Where was Thelma? Shannon was certain she had told her she needed her there by six. She decided to give her a call. Voice mail picked it up on the fourth ring.

"Thelma, this is Shannon. It's six thirty-nine AM on Tuesday July twentieth. I'm not sure if you forgot I needed you at the Dallas office by six, but please give me a call and let me know when you'll be here."

Shannon disconnected the call and stared out the window. It was completely unlike Thelma to be late for anything, ever. Shannon hoped she was all right and hadn't gotten into an accident or anything.

Shannon turned to address the gentle knock on her door. It was Kathy.

"Come on in. Have a seat, but at the table," Shannon instructed.

"As you may have expected, I found no case law that set precedent for a case of this proportion. There are various smaller cases regarding Medicare fraud, but no one has ever gone after the group purchasing organizations before," Kathy shared.

"Well, there's a first time for everything. No one had slain a giant until David did. We'll just have to make the precedent then," Shannon said as she glanced at her watch.

"True. Where's Thelma? I wanted to ask her who all from her office is on this case. I have some ideas I want to research, but it will take a couple of us."

"Great question. It's not like her to be late. I hope she's all right. My gut is saying something happened," a worried Shannon said.

"Do you want me to call her?" Kathy asked.

"I already did. I guess it wouldn't hurt, though. Go ahead and call her again. I need a cup of coffee," Shannon said as she pitched her phone to Kathy.

Kathy found Thelma's number and hit redial. After four rings it went straight to voicemail. Kathy hung up and tried again. Maybe Thelma overslept and her phone wasn't in the room, so she couldn't hear it. That had happened to Kathy before. Or maybe Thelma was asleep and thought she was only dreaming the phone was ringing. That had also happened to Kathy before. She decided to hang up and call again. This time the phone was answered on the second ring by Lilly.

"Hello," came the half-awake greeting.

"Hi. This is Kathy Carraway. Is this Thelma?"

"No. This is her daughter, Lilly. She must have forgotten her phone," the girl groggily said.

"So, she left already?" Kathy queried.

"I guess. She was supposed to be at work super early."

"Yes. That's why I'm calling. She never made it here."

"Hmmmm.  Hang on.  Let me check."

Lilly had to squint.  Her eyes were still not focused.  It was too early to be awake, so they protested, as did the rest of her body.  She ached like a fifty-year-old woman.  Slowly she put one foot in front of the other and looked around.

Her mother's keys were still on the table next to where the phone had been.  She must have overslept.  Lilly dutifully ran up the stairs to let Thelma know she had a call.  When she opened the bedroom door, no one was there.

"Mom!"

Lilly looked in her mother's bathroom.  The shower wasn't wet and the clothes she had laid out for work still hung on the back of the door.  The bed was a mess.  The covers were down on the floor, and one of the pillows was down by the foot of the bed instead of the head where it belonged.  For some reason, this sent a shiver up Lilly's spine.

"Mom!" she called again.

Lilly exited the bedroom and checked the hall bathroom. No one there. She walked to her own room to check. She'd fallen asleep on the couch. Maybe her mom had crashed in her room? She briskly walked down the hallway and peeked her head into the room. The neatly made bed said no one had slept there since Lilly had two nights ago.

Lilly checked the guest bedroom. Nothing. She held the phone receiver up to her ear and asked Kathy to give her just a second to get her mother on the line. Then she walked back downstairs and searched the house, including the garage. The car was parked there, but no Thelma.

"I'm sorry. I've literally looked over the entire house, but she's not here. Who is this again? I'll have her call you as soon as I see her."

"Hang on a second."

Kathy passed the phone to Shannon.

"Hey, Lilly. This is Shannon. Your mom was supposed to meet me and she is usually a half hour early. You don't know where she went?"

"No. I don't. It's weird because her car is still here."

A sense of dread hit Shannon. She didn't know where Thelma was, but she suddenly started to feel that something happened. She hid this from Lilly.

"All right. Well, just have her call me back."

"Ok. I will."

Now wide awake, Lilly decided to go for a morning swim. She loved to swim but hadn't been in the pool too much lately. Her summer school course load kept her occupied.

She ran upstairs and changed into her bathing suit. She grabbed a towel out of her mother's bathroom closet. Thelma's retainer was still on the counter in its open case. That was weird. She never left home without it. She said she had paid entirely too much money to have beautiful teeth, so she would obey her orthodontist at all costs.

A little spooked, Lilly darted back downstairs. She opened the shutters to the windows that faced the back yard. It was a beautiful sunny morning, and she wanted to let the sunshine in. When she opened the last shutter, she noticed there was something in the pool. She couldn't quite make out what it was, but it looked like a sheet.

From time to time, her mother liked to wash the bed linens and hang them on a clothesline out back. Thelma said she loved the smell because it reminded her of her grandmother. Lilly didn't remember her mother hanging anything out to dry, but clearly she did and now it was floating in the pool

She eased out the back door and placed her towel on her favorite patio lounger. She slipped her flip flops off and walked near the edge of the pool. She stuck her left foot in to test the temperature. It was perfect. Warm enough to not give her a shock, but cool enough to be refreshing.

The sheet seemed to have gotten something bunched up in it. Lilly couldn't tell what, though. The sheet and whatever it was had floated to the middle of the pool. Lilly hated to just dive into the pool. She much preferred to ease her way in, inch by inch. But she knew it would be a mess if the sheet clogged up a drain or something, so she decided to just dive in and go get it.

She splashed in, just a few inches from the sheet. That is when she realized the sheet hadn't entangled debris. Her mother was entangled in the sheet. For a moment, Lilly couldn't move. She tried to scream but nothing came out. A lump in her throat prevented it.

She swam over and fought with the sheet to free her mother. Thelma began to sink a little, but continued to float. Lilly stared, transfixed. She was frozen for several minutes before a gut wrenching wail sprang forth from her lips. Then she began to scream.

She made her way to the edge of the pool and tried to climb out. She slipped and fell. She scrambled to stand, but her legs were weak. She fell down again. She looked over at her mother in the pool. She dove back in. She didn't want to leave her there alone, but she needed to call for help.

Lilly climbed out of the pool once more. She inhaled deeply and remembered something her mother always said to her in a time of crisis. Crying won't make the situation any better. Remain calm and you can have a breakdown after you handle the problem.

This memory gave Lilly the courage to walk back into the kitchen to call 911.

"911. What's your emergency?"

"I just found my mother in the swimming pool. I think someone murdered her."

CHAPTER TEN

It had been exactly one month since Thelma had turned up drowned in her swimming pool. She was only fifty-five years old. She left to grieve her memory her eighty-four-year-old mother and her twenty-two-year-old daughter. She'd had ample insurance, and a will. She'd left detailed instructions in a folder with her will regarding her wishes for her funeral. Lilly was following them to the tee, and then she stopped.

Suddenly, the funeral would no longer take place on Thursday. There would be no obituary published. There were no news stories or press releases from either the Department of Justice, or the field office in which she worked. The family would not accept visitors, and no autopsy was performed. The family also became emphatic in their assertion that Thelma's death was an accident, and not a murder.

Most disturbing to Shannon was the fact that the family decided to cremate Thelma. This disturbed most of Thelma's friends and colleagues. Thelma had always been very vocal about her disdain for cremation. She said she'd die twice if she were cremated. She used to say it seemed disrespectful to her to just burn someone up like that. Yet, this was the fate she was dealt. It just didn't make sense that Lilly was the one to authorize it. She was so close to her mother. Everyone thought she would have fulfilled her mother's wishes, but she didn't. She cremated Thelma and disappeared within the span of a week.

Shannon sat at her desk and massaged her temples. She couldn't understand why no one would investigate Thelma's death. Her superiors told her to leave it alone. The family was at peace, and a long, protracted investigation would just reveal what they already knew: It was an accident. Shannon couldn't shake the feeling that it wasn't, though.

As she stared at the mound of Novation paperwork on her desk, Shannon was reminded that this case now had two dead attorneys in its wake. Mike Weiss had died in Houston under suspicious circumstances. No one cared because he was thought to be an out of control partier who went a little overboard with his favorite illegal drug. His housekeeper told everyone he would not have "partied" while working on such a big case. Too bad no one believed her.

Now there was Thelma. Thelma Louise Quince Colbert. Found face down in her panties, bra and a sheet in her swimming pool. Her daughter initially reported the death as a possible murder. Suddenly, she decided it was an accident and that was enough that, despite being a DOJ employee, poor Thelma had no one who looked into her death. No one. This wasn't right but Shannon didn't know what to do. The fraud investigation had slowed to a semi-halt as Shannon tried to get someone to investigate Thelma's death.  It was time to light a fire under someone about Novation and Thelma.

She stared at her desk for a moment before she picked up the phone.  She quickly dialed a number.  It went straight to voicemail.  She hung up and dialed another number.  It was answered on the first ring.

"New York Times, this is Mary Walsh.  How may I help you?"

"Hi, Mary.  It's Shannon. Shannon Ross over at the U S Attorney's Office in Dallas.  How are you doing?"

Mary Williams Walsh smiled and sat a little straighter when she heard who was on the line.  She had spoken back and forth to this attorney, and had written a jaw dropping piece about the fraud going on in the healthcare industry.  Shannon, however, would not allow her to publish it when they first talked.  She told her she'd let her know when.

"It's time," Shannon said.

"You sure?"

"Positive."

Shannon disconnected the call and looked at the clock on the wall. She calculated that in a little more than fourteen hours, she'd have some people more scared than they already were, as they should be. She smiled. Then she got back to the business of the papers on her desk, and waited.

## CHAPTER ELEVEN

The next morning, Saturday August 21st, the New York Times printed an article with a headline that proclaimed "Wide U S Inquiry Into Purchasing For Health Care." Shannon smiled as she sipped her coffee and read it. This was just the beginning. She planned to lob several more salvo rounds before it was over.

On Monday morning, Shannon called Kathy into her office.

"I need you to go over to the Fort Worth office and pick up every single file that Thelma had touched in the last year and a half. Every single one."

"What if they don't just hand them over to me?" Kathy asked.

"Oh, they will. Take this."

Shannon handed Kathy a subpoena.

"I hope you don't have to use it, but if you do, so be it," Shannon said as she scribbled down a name on a sheet of paper. "When you get there, ask for him.

I'm pretty sure he'll give you what you need without the subpoena."

"Ok. I'll be back soon."

Kathy bit her lip as she headed out the door. As she made her way to the parking lot, she could think of nothing but the horror Thelma's daughter must have dealt with when she found her mother. Thelma seemed like such a great mother, nothing like her own had been.

Kathy approached her car in the parking lot and noticed something on the windshield of her car. She slowed her gait, and narrowed her eyes. What she saw looked like a shirt, and it was wrapped, purposefully, around her windshield wiper. Her gut suddenly ached. Jake used to call it In-tube-ition. He said it was your intuition kicking in because of something scary you'd seen on the boob tube, also known as television. Kathy hurriedly jumped into the car and locked her doors. She had not bothered to remove the item from the windshield before she spun out of the parking lot.

As she turned left toward the freeway, that is when she noticed the sedan that followed her. She made a quick right and headed away from where she really wanted to go. So did the car. She did a U-Turn at the next corner. So did the car. Kathy's heartbeat accelerated. Sweat poured from her brow. Her hands began to shake. Kathy suddenly slammed on her brakes.

The black sedan veered quickly around her, then stopped in front of her. The man on the passenger's side hopped out of the car and walked toward Kathy. She fumbled for her phone, but her hands shook too much. She dropped it as quickly as she found it. She locked her door and closed her eyes. He knocked on her window.

"M'am. You dropped this. I just wanted to give it back to you," he said.

Kathy opened her eyes and saw his outstretched hand.

He held her work badge. She let her window down. Then she froze in place. She was unable to utter a word. Her in-tube-ition had kicked in, at full force. Meanwhile, the scent of the man's expensive cologne slowly smothered her.

"You dropped it in the parking lot."

"Thank you so much," Kathy stammered, somewhat ashamed of the panic that had almost overcome her.

After a few moments passed and Kathy had not taken what he offered, the man tossed the badge through Kathy's window and headed back to his own vehicle. Kathy watched him. She took in every detail about him. His slow gait, his salt and pepper grey hair, and his chiseled jawline. She figured he was about six feet tall, and more or less a hundred and ninety pounds. His haircut was a hip and trendy style, and his clothes screamed that they were expensive. She watched as he drove away. 8HUSLE. For some reason she read his license plate out loud as a word. She did this a few times, until her hands no longer shook, and her breathing had slowed. Nothing could be heard except the faint sound of Kathy's engine as it hummed. Kathy burst into laughter. She chided herself for being paranoid.

She put the car into gear and started to pull away. That's when she noticed the shirt still attached to her windshield. She shook her head and laughed again. What was she so paranoid about? She did work downtown after all. Maybe a transient or some kid pulling a prank had left the shirt there. She put the car in park, and hopped out to remove the shirt. As she unraveled it, she saw the shirt had a note pinned to it.

*Miss Carraway: Please have someone check this shirt. I found it at the scene of Thelma Quince Colbert's death. PD crime lab wouldn't process it.*

Kathy balled up the shirt and tossed it and the note onto her passenger seat.  She nervously looked around, and when she was sure no one was watching, she hopped back into her driver's seat and drove away as quickly as she could.

As she entered the freeway, Kathy glanced repeatedly into her rear view mirror.  She wondered if the man who returned her badge had been the one to leave the shirt.  She could think of nothing else all the way to Thelma's office.  When she finally arrived at the Ft. Worth office, Kathy paused for just a moment.  She toyed with the idea of calling Shannon, then decided against it.  She'd talk to her about the shirt in person.  Some things were just too strange to relay in a phone call, she decided.

As she opened her door to exit the vehicle, Kathy noticed the black sedan again.  It was parked three spots down from her.  She confirmed the license plate.  8HUSLE.  She could see the driver clearly.  He had red hair, probably mid-forties, and heavy set. In the passenger's seat sat the same man who had approached Kathy earlier about her identification badge. He nodded in her direction and smiled, an acknowledgement that he saw her as she checked him out. She pulled her legs back into her car and shut the door.

She breathed heavily for a few moments before she pulled out her phone and called Shannon. When Shannon answered, Kathy dispensed with cursory hellos and filled her in on every detail of what had transpired. Shannon sat quiet for just a moment.

"You can't show fear. Haven't I taught you anything?"

Kathy was more frightened now. Sweat fell from her brow onto the back of her hand. She stared at it for a moment. For a split second, she wished Jake were there.

"Yes, you've taught me a lot.  I really don't know if they are good guys, or bad guys.  If they put the shirt on my windshield, why follow me?  If they didn't, why follow me?"

"It could just be a coincidence.  They didn't actually follow you.  It sounds like they were there before you arrived."

Kathy thought about this.  She glanced over at the men.  At that moment, an attorney she recognized, Bruce Graham walked over to the sedan and greeted the driver.  The passenger came around and shook Bruce's hand.  Then the driver got out and the three stood in the parking lot chatting.  Kathy felt a small sense of relief.  Bruce was a proverbial choir boy and unlikely to keep company with miscreants.

"Shannon, I'm good.  I think you're right.  Just a coincidence.  I'll get the files and be back soon."

"Ok.  See ya then."

Kathy exited the car and waved a greeting to Bruce as she headed into the building.  He smiled and motioned for her to come over.

"Kathy Carraway here works for DOJ over in our Dallas office.  She's new to the US Attorney's Office.  Kathy, meet Vince Caldoa and Dusty Giancana.  They are from DC.  They work with White House Counsel Alberto Gonzales."

"Good day, Ms. Carraway," Vince, the red head, said.

"Nice to meet you," Dusty said, as Kathy once again almost suffocated on his cologne.

"They just left a briefing over at your office in Dallas.  I'm surprised you didn't run into each other over there," Bruce said.

"Actually, we did see each other briefly in the parking lot.  Miss Carraway dropped her ID and I returned it to her."

"That was much appreciated, by the way," Kathy smiled.

"No problem.  Anything for an attorney who is bold enough to try to bring the healthcare industry down."

The remark froze Kathy in her tracks.  Where did he get this information from?  Did his remark insinuate going after the healthcare industry was her idea?  She suddenly felt afraid again.

"I work at the White House.  I, um, hear things," Dusty said with a smirk.

They all chuckled and Kathy bid them farewell. She made her way into the building.  She quickly found Thelma's office and her point of contact.  Kathy was surprised that everything was already neatly bundled and seemed to be waiting on her.

"Did Shannon tell you I was coming?" Kathy asked the attorney who helped her.

"She didn't have to.  I knew Thelma quite well, and I know Shannon.  I figured it was just a matter of time, and here you are."

Kathy smiled stiffly.  She loaded her briefcase with as many files as possible.  The rest overflowed from her arms like water about to spill from an over filled cup.  Just as she was ready to leave, Brett Manning walked in.

"What's going on here?" he scowled, more so than asked.

Kathy quickly explained she'd been sent by Shannon to gather up Thelma's files so that she could close out the most pressing matters.

"Well, I'm not letting those files walk out of here.  I have my orders."

"No problem," Kathy sneered.  She reached a hand into her purse while she carefully held on to the files. She fished around blindly for a moment until she found what she was looking for.

"Here you go. I have my orders, too. Have a nice day," Kathy said as she tossed the subpoena for the files in his direction.

Brett caught the document and looked it over briefly before he accepted defeat.

"Just keep us abreast of what's going on with those," he ordered, a last ditch attempt to assert his authority as interim Chief of the Civil Enforcement Unit of the Fort Worth US Attorney's Office.

He had competed with Thelma for the position years ago, but she'd won. He'd never forgiven her. She'd somehow wounded his ego by being the better qualified candidate. He'd given her hell ever since. Clearly, even in death, he was still determined to do so.

"Thanks for the help," Kathy said to the clerk.

Then, head and eyes straight forward, she marched out of the building. She couldn't wait to get back to the safety of her own office, she thought as she plopped down in her car. She kicked her heels off and drove barefoot back to her office. Something about driving with no shoes on lessened her stress level.

She reached to turn the radio on as she cruised down the freeway toward her office. That's when she noticed the shirt was no longer on the passenger seat where she'd left it. In its place was a tiny box that made a nearly imperceptible ticking sound.

Kathy's heart began to race again. She looked into her rear view mirror. She had a feeling the sedan may have followed her. She didn't see it, so she pulled over to the shoulder of the freeway. She grabbed her phone and hopped out to call the police. As she shut the door, she thought about the files. She quickly yanked the door open and scooped them up.

She moved thirty feet to the rear of the vehicle. She had read somewhere that was a safe distance to be if a vehicle exploded. Then she remembered her purse on the front seat. Just as she took the first step toward the car to get it, the car exploded.

Kathy froze in place, but only for a split second. She hurriedly dialed 911 and outlined the situation. She was told first responders would be on scene in just a few moments. She hung up and dialed Shannon.

"I'm on my way," was all Shannon said before she disconnected the call.

The next hour or so was a blur. The firefighters arrived first, and extinguished the smoldering pile of ashes that used to be Kathy's car. The police officers arrived moments later. The Crime Scene Unit and detectives arrived shortly after them. They all told her to be careful.

Once the remains of Kathy's car had been towed and cleared away, Shannon whisked her away.

"Where are we going?"

"The first stop is to rent a car. I checked mine and didn't see anything, but you never know," Shannon shared.

"And the second stop?" Kathy queried.

"I think a road trip is in order. We have some research to do, and someone here doesn't want us to do it," Shannon sighed.

Kathy felt this to be true, but once she heard it said aloud, it unnerved her. She nervously clasped her hands together. What if they were being watched? What if there was no place to hide?

"I think it's an admirable thing you are doing, looking into Thelma's cases, trying to see what really happened to her. I hope I can learn to be as good of a person as you are one day," Kathy confided.

Shannon took her eyes off the road for a split second to look Kathy in the eyes.

"You don't *learn* to be a good person. You simply have to *be* a good person. We all have a little bit of humanity in our hearts, and we develop it with every act we take toward making the world a better, kinder place."

Kathy nodded her head and turned to look out the window.  The sun was setting as they pulled into the Hertz rental lot fifteen minutes later.  Shannon told Kathy to wait there, and she'd be right back.

Ten minutes passed, and Kathy started to feel nervous.  Just then, Shannon whistled for her and motioned for her to follow.  Kathy grabbed the files and headed in Shannon's direction.  She suddenly remembered she had no identification, as her purse had burned up in the car.  She reminded Shannon.

"No worries.  Fortunately for us, you hadn't picked up your DOJ issued passport for official government travel yet.  I picked it up for you."

Kathy smiled a toothy grin.  Once again, Shannon had thought of everything.

"Here it is," Shannon motioned toward a tiny Ford Escort.

"Well, at least it will be good on gas," Kathy remarked.

"More importantly, it's non-descript and perfect for people on the run," Shannon quipped back.

The sun was beginning to set, and it had been a long day.  Both women were tired, but they knew there was work to be done.  The files that Kathy clutched were a reminder of this.  Kathy's scorched sleeve was another stark reminder of the ominous work that lie ahead.

"I was thinking I'd head toward Houston. They say dead men don't talk, but maybe Mike Weiss left us some tangible clues we can use," Shannon shared.

"That attorney?  Do you really think he was on to something?"

"I've got two dead attorneys and they were both looking into the same folks.  If it walks like a duck...," Shannon started.

"…it's a duck," Kathy finished.

The two women high fived each other, then settled in

for their long ride.

# CHAPTER TWELVE

Kathy rolled out of bed with a catlike stretch. They'd found a very shabby chain motel that looked as if it hadn't had many guests since the seventies. Well, at least guests that weren't prostitutes. Or people on the run. The irony made Kathy giggle to herself.

She looked over and noticed that Shannon wasn't in the other bed, and this made her panic a little. She looked out the window of their third floor room and realized the car wasn't there. Had Shannon left her? Kathy leapt to her feet and tossed on a blouse and slacks Shannon had given her the night before. She slipped on her shoes and headed toward the door. For a fleeting moment, Kathy hoped Shannon really had left her. Then she'd have an excuse to get on a plane to Anywhere and get away from this nightmare case. Then she came back to reality. She'd have to flee later. For now, she needed to see if Shannon was outside someplace.

Just as Kathy reached for the door knob, Shannon walked in with a bag that smelled like it contained breakfast.

"Where are you headed, kiddo?  We've got work to do!" Shannon quipped as she put the food on the desk.

"I was going to look for you…," Kathy stammered.

"Sit.  We have work to do," Shannon gently ordered, as she handed a bacon biscuit and orange juice to Kathy.

When the women finally took a break to look up from their mound of research, nearly twenty hours had passed.  They were tired and hungry, but they pressed forward.  Shannon wanted to find out exactly how nasty the serpent was that they were dealing with so she could make a plan of attack.

"Do any restaurants deliver right now?  I have to eat something," Kathy announced as she pushed her chair back and stood to stretch.

"Grab that menu over there and see," Shannon said as she pointed toward the dresser.

Kathy scanned the document for a moment before she almost shouted "Yes!  Breakfast delivery starts in five more minutes."

Then Shannon looked up.

"Wait.  It's breakfast time?"

"Yep.  Nearly six a.m."

"No wonder I'm starving."

"Give me just a sec to order.  What do you want.  Your usual Hazelnut coffee, lots of creamer, no sugar and an oatmeal with brown sugar on the side?"

Shannon blew a kiss in appreciation that Kathy remembered.  Kathy placed the order and returned to her place at the desk.  She looked at the sea of paperwork before her, and noticed a detail that caught her attention.

"Shannon, check this out."

Shannon stood up and took the single sheet of paperwork from Kathy's hand. She walked toward the window and rubbed her head slowly. The desire to sleep was slowly taking over her ability to process all the information that still needed to be waded through. As Shannon read the first sentence, her skin tightened and her flesh began to crawl. Each word left a bitter tang in her mouth. A vein began to throb visibly in her forehead. Her lips pulled back, and she bared her teeth.

"The White House has ties to this?" Shannon seethed, then turned to look out the window.

There was a thunderous knock at the door.

"Delivery!" came the baritone announcement on the other side of the door.

Kathy opened the door.  There stood Fred Jones.  As Kathy recalled, he was a US Marshall who worked in her building, not a hotel delivery man.

"Fred?"

Shannon spun around.  Her eyes narrowed, and she rubbed her chin.  Fred stepped inside the room and closed the door.  Shannon motioned for him to have a seat at the table.

"There's no time for that.  You ladies have to get out of here.  Your lives are in danger."

Shannon felt her breath quicken.  She suddenly had a knot in her stomach.  She maintained her game face, though.  She looked Fred directly in his eyes for a few moments.

"Well tell us something we don't know.  How'd you come by this information?  Why are you here?"

"The better question is how did you know we were here?" Kathy interjected.

"When you took on this case, and wouldn't let it go, you became a target."

"What case are you speaking of?" Shannon asked.

Fred smiled slightly. He looked at the floor for a split second. Then he shot Shannon a glance that said he was on her side. He tapped his fingertips together for a few more seconds. After several more seconds, he spoke.

"Shannon, you allowed Thelma to take on the entire healthcare system of the United States. You can't be so naïve to think there isn't a lot on the line for the players involved. You have to know they will go to any length to protect their stake. That lawyer's death in Houston proves that."

Shannon weighed the danger level of the situation. Her breath quickened ever so slightly. The thump of her heartbeat increased. She could feel the adrenaline as it circulated in her system. She leaned into Fred as she asked her question.

"How did you know we were here?"

"Let's just say it is in Novation's interest to know what you are up to at all times. Do you understand what I'm saying?"

Shannon bit the inside of her lip and rubbed absently at her arms. Her chest began to tingle. Her thoughts scrambled and raced wildly in her head. She laughed nervously before she asked her next question.

"So, are you our knight in shining armor, or theirs?"

"Theirs. But after what they did to Thelma, well… Listen. Just get out of here. You truly don't have much time."

"Who did what to Thelma?" Kathy asked.

"She was a threat. She was eliminated. You are a threat, and you will be eliminated, too, if you don't stop snooping. Now get out of here," Fred ordered before he departed the room.

As the door clicked behind him, gunfire erupted in the hallway. Shannon put her fingers up to her lips as a signal for Kathy to be quiet. Then she pointed to the large air duct at the bottom of the wall near the bathroom entry.

"We're going to crawl into that that?"

"Yes, if you want to live," Shannon whispered with authority.

Fortunately, the metal outer piece lifted out with no problem, as it had no screws. Shannon crawled through first, then reached back and yanked Kathy along. It was dark, and Kathy could scarcely see in front of her face. That didn't prevent her from keeping pace with Shannon as they made their way through the ventilation system at an Olympian's pace. When they reached the light that beckoned to them at the end of the ventilation system's tunnel, Shannon began to kick until the cover of the opening came open. She peeked out. They were several stories up, but could definitely make the jump, she surmised.

"We're going to jump, and then run like hell," Shannon told a petrified Kathy.

Kathy nodded that she understood, then clasped on to Shannon's outstretched hand.

"One, two, three!" Shannon cried as they jumped. They hit the landing of the staircase below with a thud. Kathy struggled to a standing position. Shannon had already jumped up, and was in a defensive stance, taking a quick note of her surroundings.

"This is going to hurt tomorrow," Kathy mumbled to no one in particular.

Just then, the landing began to shake. The ground beneath them began to buckle. The stairs started to crumble.

"Run!" Shannon commanded.

Before they could get to the bottom of the stairs, the walls of the hotel burst open. Flames spewed in every direction. Shannon was thrown one way, and Kathy the other, yet they managed to keep one another in sight. Shannon crawled slowly toward Kathy, who was covered in blood.

"I'm good. Let's just get out of here, Shannon," Kathy mouthed.

A whistle to the left caught their attention. It was Fred. He beckoned them toward the getaway car. They didn't hesitate to oblige.

"I thought you had gotten yourself killed in there," Shannon chided.

"Absolutely not. I knocked out a few people and then I blew the building up before the real bad guys get here."

"The *real* bad guys? They seemed pretty real to me!" Kathy joked as she followed Shannon's lead and hopped into the car. She squeezed into the front seat, despite them being of the bucket variety.

Fred sped away just as the gunfire erupted again. Kathy wanted to look back at the scene unfolding behind them but she was too frightened. Fred startled her away from her thoughts by tossing a handgun into her lap.

She looked up in time to see Shannon locking and loading her own handgun.

"Shannon, take the wheel!" Fred yelled as he dove from the vehicle.

Like a basketball thrown for the three point shot, he sailed through the air, bounced into a roadside bush, then rolled right back into the middle of the excitement. Kathy squeezed her eyes closed. She didn't want to see anymore. What she heard was more than enough.

"Shoot his tires out," Shannon calmly commanded.

Kathy opened her eyes and took a peek in the passenger side mirror.  A sports car of some variety increased speed and came too close for comfort.  Fred was no longer visible.

"How am I supposed to do that?"

"Lean out of your window, take aim and fire. Like your life depends on it.  Oh, that's right.  It does!"

Kathy said a quick prayer to herself, then stared at the weapon in her lap.  As she was about to say she couldn't do it, a bullet whizzed by her right ear.  That was just what she needed to ignite her courage.

She looked at the weapon's magazine.  It was a ten round clip. She knew she didn't need that many. Her anger would direct her shot to its target.  She took the safety off, eyed her target in the mirror, then leaned out and fired.

The car flipped and sailed through the air as if it had wings.  As it touched earth again, it burst into flames.  Kathy's mouth fell open.  She touched her throat gently.  Then she let out a bark of laughter.

"Did you see that, Shannon!"

"I told you that you were perfect for this job," Shannon said with a wink.

She took a hard right at the intersection, and left all signs of trouble behind them.

# CHAPTER THIRTEEN

It had been nearly forty-eight hours since Kathy and Shannon had escaped Hell with their lives intact.  The duo had elected to hide away in a cheap family owned motel, in a town inhabited by only a handful of people.  They'd managed to finish their research project.  They were even able to do some additional research on the attorney in Houston who had died seemingly as a result of this case.

"So, there's enough evidence for an indictment?" Kathy asked.

"Yep.  I'll sign the indictments tomorrow when we get back to the office."

"I guess I'll start prepping the warrants."

"It shouldn't take too long to knock out all the paperwork.  And then I'll let you enjoy a long weekend."

"Long weekend?  Tomorrow's Friday."

"Yes, long weekend. You'll actually get Saturday and Sunday off, so much longer than most," Shannon teased.

The two giggled, and then decided to retire for a well-deserved slumber. The next morning was uneventful. They ate a hearty breakfast of oatmeal, toast and blueberries. Lots of blueberries. Blueberries reminded Kathy of Jake. It had been so many years since she had consumed one of her brother's fabulous blueberry smoothies, but she found comfort in remembering them whenever she ate a fresh berry. If only Jake was still here to listen to the events of the last few days, she thought.

The drive back to the office was just as uneventful as the rest of the morning. As they pulled into a visitor spot, rather than Shannon's marked spot, both women took in their surroundings. Only sun and southern charm seemed to await them. As they walked into the building, a familiar sight caught their attention. Fred Jones stood at his post, as always.

He saw the ladies, and flashed one of his brilliant smiles.

"Good morning Ms. Ross. Ms. Carraway. If I don't see you when you leave, have a great weekend!"

"You, too, Fred," came Shannon's reply.

Kathy could only stand with her mouth open, and offer a blank stare. Had she taken a job in the Twilight Zone? What was going on? She felt her sense of safety and security creep down just a notch.

Shannon caught the look and whispered to Kathy "Don't worry. I have some magic tricks up my sleeve, too."

Kathy momentarily longed for the safety of less pay and longer hours with Bubba back at the Chicken Shack. Then she remembered she was here to make a difference in the world. Chicken was great, but it didn't impact the moral conscience of America in the same way. She also realized she looked ridiculous in the feathered hat and neon shirt she used to be forced to wear. The thought made her laugh aloud.

"And why do you find so much humor in this?" Shannon asked, amused.

Kathy snapped back to reality.

"I don't. Just…thinking. That's all."

"Ok. Well, let's do our thinking upstairs. See you later, Fred."

Fred smiled again, and nodded in acknowledgement. He watched as the women made their way to the elevator. Kathy took note of this, and shuddered.

"Why is Fred watching us? That's creepy," Kathy confided once they were alone inside the elevator.

"I have no idea, and I am too worn out to care right now. At this moment, all I want to do is get in my office, sign these indictments and get the warrants processed."

"Yeah, me, too," Kathy admitted.

The elevator signaled they had reached their destination, and the doors opened. To their surprise, and Shannon's chagrin, there stood Alberto Gonzales.

"Shan Non Ross!" he exclaimed, in his usual annoying manner.

Hearing this made Kathy cringe. Shannon had to restrain herself from spitting on him.

"Alberto. What brings you to our office on this fine Friday morning?"

"Just making sure everything's running like a well-oiled machine. Making sure everything's in good repair, and you all don't need an exterminator."

"Exterminator?" Shannon asked.

"You know, for the pests that can sometimes pop up in big buildings like these. A lot of these old Dallas buildings have a problem with rats. I wouldn't want you all to have to deal with such creatures. I'm willing to spare no expense to make sure we have the cleanest work environment possible. I'm sure you share this philosophy, right?"

"Oh, Albert. I can tell you are a city boy. I'm a country girl, so let me share something with you. Rats are very strong and survive, even in the most dire circumstances. They aren't that easy to get rid of," Shannon sneered.

Her cold eyes said she was not to be messed with today. She assumed a wide stance. Her chest thrust out. Kathy stiffened, unsure of whether to prepare for a fist fight, or flee.

"Excuse me. You're blocking the elevator," Lacey Griffins said to the group.

Lacey was an attorney in the Organized Crime Unit. On most days, however, it was difficult to distinguish her from a two-dollar trollop, as Shannon often said. Kathy quickly eyed Lacey from head to toe.

Today was no different.  She looked like a two-dollar trollop.

"Oh, excuse us.  Shannon, come on.  We have a few things to knock out before the end of the day," Kathy said as she gently guided Shannon by the arm. As they made their way down the hall, Kathy glanced over her shoulder.  Alberto Gonzales remained positioned in front of the elevator.  He was on his phone.  Kathy wondered what plot was being hatched, but she said nothing.  She kept her head and eyes straight forward all the way to Shannon's office.

"That man disgusts me!" Shannon announced as she plopped down into her chair.

"It's like he's…the devil. Just wicked. You can almost see it emanating from his soul," Kathy shared.

"Well, not today, Satan.  Not today, or any other day.  Let's get through this case, and then unseating him will be my next project before I retire."

"Retire?"

"Yes, and head to Seminary. I've already spoken to my church about becoming ordained. I was accepted at TCU for this fall. But don't worry. It's a two -year program, so I won't be out of your hair anytime soon, my friend!"

"Reverend Ross. I like it."

Shannon smiled, and then the women turned their attention to the work that loudly screamed their names. Just before six o'clock that evening, they finished their designated tasks. Indictments had been signed and announced in grand fashion to the media. The warrants were also signed. Law enforcement teams were already in motion to execute them. It looked like a good weekend was in store after all. Shannon grabbed her purse and headed down the hall to Kathy's office.

"Get out of here. Go read a book, or see a movie or something. But whatever you do, don't give this place a second thought until eight AM Monday morning," Shannon told Kathy.

"I'm already two steps ahead of you. I was just about to come tell you the same thing."

"Two great minds thinking alike again!" Shannon joked.

Kathy quickly cleared off her desk and headed out with Shannon. As they exited the building, Shannon stopped and looked at Kathy.

"Thanks for all your sticky-ta-tudy the last few days."

"My what?" Kathy curiously asked.

"You've never been to Utah?"

"Nope."

"Well, you should go. It's breathtakingly beautiful. Anyway, sticky-ta-tudy is a word locals have used since they first settled there that means sticking to your duty. Not backing out, even if you get scared. Staying with it no matter how tough and exhausting it becomes.  I appreciate you, and I'm thankful you're here."

"So am I."

The two women gave each other a sisterly hug, then went their separate ways.  They both anticipated a weekend filled with nothingness.  They were sore and fatigued both physically and mentally.  They had earned this respite from work.  They needed it to face the upcoming week refreshed.

Kathy's weekend was filled with Lifetime Original movies, a tub of ice cream, and many naps.  Despite the rest, Monday morning seemed to come in the blink of an eye.  Kathy headed in to work at her just before eight, and stuck her head in to see Shannon.  She wasn't there.  In fact, she wasn't there the entire morning.

Kathy figured Shannon had slept in one more day, but would be at work after lunch.  When Shannon missed the team briefing at one o'clock, Kathy felt something was wrong.  As the facilitator, Shannon would never miss it without letting someone know. Kathy decided to call Shannon.  She took a seat at her desk, knees tightly clasped together, and dialed.  It went straight to voicemail.

Afraid she'd seem paranoid, Kathy decided not to leave a voicemail.  She waited an hour before she called back.  Again, it went straight to voicemail. Kathy's hand went instinctively to her stomach.  The familiar pangs of dread were within her.  Sweat began to bead upon her forehead as she tried to calm herself.

"You don't look so good," Dusty Giancana quipped from the doorway.

"I'm fine.  What can I do for you?" a startled Kathy asked Dusty, who, according to his name badge, held the position of Alberto Gonzales' right hand man.

She silently examined him for a moment.  He was a familiar face. She just couldn't place why.  Then she remembered. The parking lot debacle, as she now called it.

"I was looking for your boss, Shannon. Is she around?"

"She's tied up right now. Can I help you with something?"

"Nah. It can wait. Just let her know I'm looking for her, ok?"

"Absolutely."

Kathy nearly ran to close her door as Dusty left. She took a seat at her desk, and rocked almost imperceptibly. Her hands trembled just a bit as she took out her cell phone to call Shannon again. The call, once more, went straight to voicemail. Kathy's head drooped and she hunched forward in her chair. Her mind raced. She straightened up, and dialed another number.

"Dallas Police Department. This is Detective Seay speaking. How may I help you, sir or m'am?"

"Hello, James.  This is Kathy Carraway.  How are you?"

"Old and wishing I were out fishing instead.  How are you?  Good to hear from you."

"I'm well, but a little worried about a mutual friend of ours, Shannon Ross.  She didn't show up for work today.  It's probably no big deal.  We had a pretty stressful caseload last week, but I'd appreciate it if you could just drive by her house and make sure she is all right."

"She didn't call in?  You're sure she's not using a sick day?"

"No, she didn't call in.  No one's heard from her all day, and that's not like her."

"Yeah, that's absolutely not like her.  I'm still trying to recover from her 'Courtesy Calls Work Wonders' lecture I got five or six years ago when I called in sick and missed a court appearance.  I'll have a unit go check it out."

"I'd prefer you go. That way, if it's nothing, we haven't set off a bunch of false alarms."

"What's in it for me," Detective Seay asked flirtatiously.

Kathy frowned. This was a serious matter. There was no time for playing dating games. She cleared her throat loudly, to convey the seriousness of the matter at hand.

"Honor and selfless service are in it for you. If she's sick or something, I'm sure you'll feel much better knowing you could come to her aid. If she's fine, well, you'll have the satisfaction of knowing you came to my aid at a time when I felt like a damsel in distress," Kathy said sternly.

"Ok. What's the address?"

"Fifty-eight-seventy-one Runyon Court."

"I'll get back to you as soon as I make contact."

"Thank you."

"Don't worry. I am sure she's fine."

"I certainly hope so."

Kathy disconnected the call, and stood to pace the floor. She took several deep breaths in an effort to calm herself. She sauntered over to the window and peeked out. Nothing but sunshine and the usual bustle of people headed to or leaving the Federal Court House across the street.

She sluggishly took a seat at her desk, then twirled in her chair for a moment. Her mind overflowed with flashbacks of the last few days. Her brow furrowed at the thought of their unpleasantness. She buried her head in her hands as she wondered where Shannon was. After an hour or so, her phone rang.

"Hey, it's James."

"You found her? Why isn't she answering her phone? Why isn't she here at work?"

An overwhelming silence loomed. Kathy's heart sank. She did not like silence. The one thing

Detective Seay did not like about his job was having to be the bearer of bad news.  They each stewed in private torment for a few seconds.

"Kathy, I don't have good news for you."

"Well, call me when you do!" Kathy snapped before disconnecting the call.

The phone rang again immediately.

"Detective, go find Shannon."

"I already did."

There was another painful burst of silence.

"Well, tell her she can still make her last meeting of the day if she heads out right now," Kathy said, fighting back tears.

"She won't be making any more meetings, Kathy. We found her deceased in her home.  Probable suicide.  Listen, let me come by and talk to you in person about this. Homicide will handle things here at the scene."

Silence.

"Kathy, are you still on the line?"

Kathy's voice thickened and her cheeks burned. Her chest began to ache. Her eyelids felt gummy. Her body suddenly felt much older than it was. She lifted her shoulder toward her ear to support the phone while she frantically searched her desk for tissues.

"I'm here. I'm on my way to you, Detective. Stop all work on the crime scene for a moment, please. I want to see it just as she was found," Kathy in a shaky voice.

"Yes, my friend. I'll be here when you get here."

Kathy grabbed her keys and headed out the door. She stopped mid-stride and squeezed her eyes shut. Her skin tingled and she had a heavy feeling in her stomach. She felt dizzy and wanted to hide. Then she remembered Shannon. She had to continue to do her job, to embrace the concept of sticky-ta-tudy. She didn't know who did this, but she was going to find out and follow them to the ends of the earth if she had to. She was certain Shannon did not commit suicide. Justice would be served she thought as she walked out the door.

As she made her way down the corridor from her office to the elevator, Kathy got the eerie sense that she was being followed. She discreetly pulled her make-up compact from her purse and pretended to fix her lipstick in its mirror. She saw no one behind her. Relieved, she threw it back in her purse.

She quickened her pace to the elevator. When it arrived, there was a woman already inside. Kathy didn't recognize her. Whomever she was, she certainly had great taste in shoes, Kathy noted to herself as she admired the elegant Stuart Weitzman retro rose pumps.

"Good morning, m'am," the woman said.

"Mornin'."

Kathy pressed the button for the ground floor. She had that eerie feeling again. Slowly, she eyed the other woman with her peripheral vision. The lady was immersed in something on her phone and paid Kathy no mind. Inwardly, Kathy breathed a sigh of relief. She had no idea why she was being so paranoid. Well, maybe Shannon's demise had something to do with it…

The mere thought of Shannon brought forth a river of tears. Kathy quickly wiped them away and looked around to see if the other woman noticed. She hadn't. Whatever was on her phone was far more interesting. Suddenly, the elevator doors opened. They'd arrived at the ground floor.

"Have a nice day, m'am!" the mystery woman called to Kathy as she exited the elevator.

"You, too," Kathy halfheartedly replied.

The woman winked at Kathy as she exited the elevator and made a beeline for the parking lot. Kathy thought it an odd gesture, but was too preoccupied with thoughts of Shannon to care.  In fact, she was so preoccupied that she didn't notice the man hunched down in her back seat until it was too late.  Before she could react, his hands covered her nose and mouth.  The solution on the rag he held knocked her unconscious in seconds.  Once he was certain she was passed out, he calmly exited the vehicle.  He looked around before he opened the driver side door.  He shoved Kathy's lifeless body to the passenger side, then seat belted himself into the driver's seat.  He glanced in the rearview mirror.  His hair was a mess.  He smoothed the shoulder length blond locks back in place.  He told himself he needed to use more hair product next time.  Then he sped away before anyone realized something was amiss.

## CHAPTER FOURTEEN

Kathy didn't know how long she'd been unconscious, but it had been long enough that her mouth was taped and her hands were restrained with bits of cloth, fashioned into makeshift handcuffs, in front of her. She was flat on her back on a sofa that had probably seen its best days before the fall of the Berlin Wall. She tried to sit up but couldn't. Her head throbbed too badly. Her eyes were watery and her vision blurry. She blinked her eyes a few times in an effort to see her surroundings.

She could make out the silhouettes of two men sitting at a table a few feet away. One had his back turned toward her. His long black hair was piled atop his head in a man-bun. He was dressed in all black, like a Ninja pulled straight out of a Japanese anime. Man Number Two sat across the table from the first man. He wore jeans and a denim jacket. Kathy could see his blond locks were styled in a crew cut, but the rest of his features were a blur.  The two men were engrossed in conversation, so the second man paid her no mind. Kathy squeezed her eyes tight a few times to try to lessen the blurriness of her vision.  After a few seconds, her vision improved.  Though her mouth was still taped, she let out a sigh of relief.

Man Number Two heard the noise, and stopped mid-conversation.  He turned his gaze toward Kathy.  Their eyes locked for a millisecond before the man gently kicked his cohort.

"She's up," he nearly whispered.

Man Number One let his hands fall to the table, then he braced himself for a moment on the edge.

"Let's do this," Man Number Two said.

He got up and walked toward Kathy.  He seemed familiar to her.  Something about his eyes, and the way he walked.  He stopped just short of the sofa, and turned to his pal.

"Are you just going to sit there or what?"

Man Number One got up from the table. As he turned in Kathy's direction, a wave of emotion hit her. It couldn't be. Could it? She blinked a few more times to make sure her eyes did not deceive her. She turned her head toward Man Number Two, who eyed the floor rather than eye her back. Man Number One was frozen in place. Man Number Two walked back to the table and picked his Stetson hat up from the table and placed it gingerly upon his head. He touched the brim in the direction of Man Number One.

"Come on, bwoy! Let's do this!" he said as he let his gaze fall back to his hostage on the sofa.

Kathy felt like she was going to faint. That Stetson still had a few almost imperceptible spatters of blood upon it, but Kathy saw every single one of them. Man Number Two could see the wheels turn in her head, so he walked closer to her. Kathy tried to scream, but the tape muffled her cries.  Suddenly, Man Number One broke the silence.

"Kathy, Clint's not going to hurt you.  Just let him take the tape off."

When she heard his voice, she felt like she would suffocate.  Her chest tightened, her head began to spin, and her stomach ached.  She closed her eyes. This couldn't be.  She opened her eyes and saw Clint's outstretched hands.  He asked for permission to remove the tape.  She nodded consent.

Gingerly, Clint removed the tape from her mouth. Kathy held her arms out.  She wanted her cloth handcuffs removed, as well.  Clint fished around in every pocket he had until he found his Swiss Army knife.  A few careful slashes and the restraints fell to the ground.  As Kathy sat up, she eyed each man suspiciously.  Clint didn't really hold her interest. Man Number One is where her focus was.  She walked toward him and touched his face.  Her hand moved up to his hair and she undid his tidy man-bun. She ran her fingers through his hair like a car traveling the winding back roads of a mountain, familiar yet cautious. She leaned into his chest and inhaled. That's when the tears came.

"I buried you!" she cried as she moved away.

The two men froze, unsure of what to say or do.

"What the hell is going on? I want answers!" Kathy demanded.

Clint eyed Jake, still not sure of what to say. Jake pulled Kathy close to him again. It had been a decade since he'd last seen his sister and it felt comforting to hug her. He wiped the tears from her face, and then motioned toward the sofa. Kathy took a seat. Jake sat next to her. Clint nervously reclaimed his seat at the table.

"I don't understand. I buried you," Kathy declared.

"I did it for us."

Kathy was not amused.  Her face made that clear.

"Just hear him out," Clint almost begged.

"Yes, please. Just hear me out."

Kathy gestured for Jake to proceed.

"You know I liked girls and I liked to party."

"What does that have to do with why my dead brother has had me kidnapped and why said brother is no longer dead?"

"He'll get to that in a second.  Let him finish," Clint chimed in from his spot at the table.

"Yes.  Please.  Let me finish.  So, I've always liked girls and liked to party. Well, remember that night at the hospital?  The last time you saw me?"

"How could I forget?  I was in counseling for years after that night."

"Well, about six weeks before that, I'd been out partying in Deep Ellum.  I'm sure you know without me telling you how boisterous those crowds get over there."

Kathy's eyes said she knew.

"Well, the short version is I tried to break up what I thought was a bar fight. I stopped them from pumping lead into each other, but not before someone called the police and had them carted off to jail. Turns out it was fight between two drug mules. When their handler found out that his dope, his money AND his mules were gone, he came looking for me."

"And then…?" Kathy queried.

"And then I was told I would replace them. I had to start carrying their load."

"Carrying their load? How?" Kathy asked, as if she didn't already know the answer.

"Deliverin' their product," Clint clarified.

"So, I did. I wanted to tell you about it, but I just couldn't disappoint you like that. I just figured it was a one-time deal.  I'd do it, then they'd leave me alone."

"That was incredibly stupid.  But, ok.  You transported the drugs. Then what?  How did we get to today?"

Clint cleared his throat.  Jake and Kathy both looked in his direction.  He held up a glass of iced tea.

"Anyone want a drink or a snack before we continue this story?"

"No," Kathy answered with a pinched expression and heavy sigh.

She turned her attention back to Jake.

"Go ahead.  Keep talking."

"Well, it wasn't a one-time deal.  Turns out I was a lot more efficient at moving under the radar than the two goons from the bar.  They offered me two hundred and fifty thousand dollars to make two more runs up I-forty into Tennessee.  One thousand before

I left Dallas, and the rest upon delivery of the product in Tennessee."

"What happened to the money?"

"Let me get to that part. So, I drop off the stuff right outside of Nashville, in a place called Antioch. Everything is going as planned. Product switches hands. Money switches hands. I hop in the car, excited to tell you our good fortune, and then BAM!"

He clapped his hands together for effect. Kathy jumped straight up in the air. Clint bit his cheek trying to contain his laughter.

"Bam, what?" Kathy asked.

"As I drove away, the DEA snatched me up. I had a quarter million dollars in cash in my passenger seat, drug residue in the trunk, and no valid explanation of why I was leaving the home of a Sinaloa Cartel associate."

"Sinaloa Cartel! What?" Kathy shrieked.

"Apparently they had been watching this group for a year or so, and my good fortune blessed me to make that run on the very day they decided to pop them."

"But when did you have time to go to jail and I didn't notice? You're not making sense."

"You're getting ahead of me. So, I did the delivery the night they decided to move in and start making arrests. Well, the guy who had hired me was the big fish they'd been after for like ten years. Since I had a connection to him, they didn't keep me. They struck a deal instead."

"Ok…"

"The deal was basically for me to wear a wire and get the guy to incriminate himself. In exchange, they'd let me keep my freedom. So I did. But then they changed the rules. After they arrested the guy, then not only did I have to testify, but I had to agree to help them catch some other bad guys."

"Wait. They can't just change the rules of a plea agreement like that."

"Yeah, they can, if the person being offered the deal agrees.  I agreed to do it because if I worked undercover for them, and had no contact with my family or friends, they would compensate me a million dollars per year that I was a ghost."

"And about this same time, I got caught up in the same web as your brother here, and was offered the same deal," Clint said as he walked toward Kathy and plopped on the sofa.

Kathy suddenly felt weak. She sat down, too. Jake sat beside her, with his long legs stretched far out in front of him.  He hung his head for just a moment before he continued.

"We were broke. Clint was broke. So the offer of so much money was Heaven sent as far as we were concerned.  I just had no idea how to tell you."

"But then I hatched a beautiful plan," interjected a woman's voice from the bedroom.

All three heads turned toward the voice. Clint jumped to his feet and shoved his hands in his pockets. He looked intently at Jake. Tiny beads of sweat inched down his right temple.

"Come on out, doll," Clint said, as he kept his gaze fixed nervously on Jake.

"Penny?"

Kathy couldn't believe her eyes. In front of her was yet another person whose funeral she had attended, and whose loved ones she had comforted for many years. Penny came close to hug her friend, but Kathy pulled away.

"I'm in a room full of insanity. So you all hatched a plan to live footloose and fancy free with boatloads of money while the rest of us were left to wallow in our grief and pick up the pieces? Jake, I had

*No One.* Do you hear me? No one! How could you do that to me?" Kathy sobbed softly.

"It wasn't like that. I swear!" Jake pleaded.

"It sure seems like it was. Then enlighten me."

"Yes, we came up with the plan to fake our deaths, but I was supposed to be able to call you right away and let you know what was happening."

"Wait. The whole hospital was in on this? The police? The funeral home? Everyone?"

"Pretty much," Jake assured her. "I told you, I got hemmed up by the DEA. They have some serious strings they can pull when they need to. But like I said, I was supposed to be able to call you right away, but I couldn't. One of the cartel chiefs got wind of the deal we struck, so we had to lay low and my handler, if you will, wouldn't let me jeopardize the case we were working. A successful takedown of that drug ring meant she'd get the promotion she'd had her eyes on in the U S Attorney's Office for quite some time."

"So Thelma, our handler, got the position.  But then she talked us into helping with one more gig.  By this time, six years had already passed and we were itching to get home, but  she promised to double the money if we kept at it on one more case," Penny elaborated.

"Thelma.     Thelma Quince Colbert?" a credulous Kathy asked.

"Yep."

"Hold on.  So she's alive, too?" Kathy asked as her eyes darted around the room in search of another person risen from the dead.

"No, she's not.  She's really gone.  This case she was working on was bigger than anything you can ever imagine.  The players have a lot to lose, and she was getting too close to exposing them.  Especially Gonzales.  He has the most to lose," Jake explained.

"Gonzales who?" Kathy questioned as the pit of her stomach ached.

"The current Counsel to the White House. Our recently elected Attorney General of the United States of America," came Jake's reply.

Kathy's mouth fell open. Her fingers touched her parted lips as an almost inaudible gasp escaped her mouth. Her skin tingled and her already heavy stomach felt heavier. Her breathing was suspended briefly while she collected her thoughts.

"What does Alberto Gonzales have to do with any of this?" she managed to say.

"He's got everything to do with this. Healthcare and drugs go hand in hand," Clint pointed out.

"Yes, everyone knows Big Pharma and the healthcare industry are in bed together, but what does Alberto Gonzales have to do with this?" Kathy demanded.

"He's the biggest fish, Kath," Jake said with a sigh.

Kathy grimaced and rubbed her chin.  Her eyes narrowed and her eyebrows squished together.  Her chest tightened and she began to sweat.  She repeated back what had just been said to her.

"He's the biggest fish."

"Yes, he is," Jake confirmed.

"I still don't understand what our healthcare case has to do with illegal drug activity and why Thelma is dead and you are alive."

"Kathy, illegal drugs have everything to do with your case.  The real money for those healthcare companies comes from the drug trade.  They pump people full of meth, heroin, cocaine and then offer addiction treatment services.  Trillions of dollars a year are made on that. Then the pay to play scam simply helps keep their partner facilities happy and feeling like they are making fistfuls of legitimate money, so, of course, they aren't going to ever ask any questions or dig into anything. The supervisors and docs and nurses think they are really living out their Hippocratic Oath to do no harm," Jake said.

"And it was all good until a slighted entrepreneur out of Houston wasn't invited to the party," Clint added.

"They tried to pay him off, but he wasn't interested.  He had a great product and he wanted people to know about it.  He wanted to make an impact, not a dollar," Penny shared.

"This is why there's a trail of dead attorneys?" Kathy incredulously asked.

"Bingo.  Now you're getting it," Clint almost screamed.

"Was it you guys that left that shirt on my windshield?"

"Yes. We wanted you to test the shirt and find Gonzales' DNA so you could make the link yourself," Jake confessed.

"Well, someone wanted to make sure I didn't do that. I'll tell you that story later. But I have another question."

"Yeah?" Clint responded.

"Is Shannon dead for real, or is that just a lie, too?"

"I was wondering when you'd get around to thinking of me," a familiar voice said from the bedroom.

"Sha-"

Before Kathy could finish her sentence, Shannon appeared. She squeezed in the small space between Kathy and Jake. The women hugged. Relief filled the air.

"Shannon! I thought you were dead! What is going on?" Kathy cried.

"What's going on is I'm about to bring down a villain, and you're going to help me."

The gleam returned to Kathy's eye. A sense of calm filled her spirt. Her muscles began to relax again. She leaned in to hear Shannon's next words.

"Tomorrow, you will go to work and play the role of grieving colleague all morning. At noon, you're going to hold a press conference."

"Press conference about what?"

"I'm one of the most competent U S Attorneys to ever grace the job. I don't just turn up dead and no one makes a statement, or threatens a thorough investigation."

"Oh. Right. Ok. So I hold this press conference, and then?"

"Well, all the attorneys will think your purpose for gathering the press is to make a statement regarding my death. What you are actually going to do is name one more indicted individual: Alberto Gonzales. Then waltz back into your office and wait for all holy hell to break loose," Shannon declared with a playful wink.

## CHAPTER FIFTEEN

Kathy stepped off the elevator and headed to her office a full hour before anyone else would be in the building. She wore the appropriate black suit, updo hairstyle and minimal jewelry in order to properly convey a mood filled with sorrow due to the loss of a colleague, mentor and friend. It was no secret that she and Shannon were close, so she had to play the part convincingly.

She'd arrived early so she could go through the paperwork one last time. As Shannon had taught her, she wanted to have it all committed to memory and be prepared to launch nuclear rounds at the appropriate parties. Reading the indictment against Alberto Gonzales made her shake with excitement.

*Count 1*

*The Grand Jury Charges:*

*That between March 1, 1992 and November 14, 2019, in Dallas, County, State of Texas,*

*ALBERTO GONZALES, defendant committed the offense of …*

She didn't need to read it again.  It was etched into her memory forever.  She looked at the clock. Bristol, one of the Major Crimes Unit attorneys would be in soon.  She decided to get one last cup of coffee before then.  She extended her body in a satisfied, catlike stretch as she rose and sauntered down the hall, coffee mug in hand.

She paused when she reached the break room. She took in the view from the window in hallway  The scenery from this nondescript area was beautiful to her. It was dignified.  It was beautiful.  It was full of history, like Dealey Plaza, yet full of modernism, too.  It represented what used to be, what was, and what might be.  Kathy thought it was a fitting view for the U S Attorneys office.  Ironic, actually.

As she entered the break room, she was startled to find Harold Penigar sipping on a cup of java.  He was Executive Assistant to Alberto Gonzales.  Kathy's head began to pound at the sight of him.  Too bad he was oblivious.

"Miss Carraway.  Good morning!  I'm so sorry for your loss," he said as he jumped to his feet after he saw her.

He extended a hand in hopes of a handshake. Kathy declined with a wrinkled nose and silence.  She quickly poured her coffee, grabbed a few hazelnut creamers and almost sprinted back down the hall to her office.  She heard Harold's footsteps behind her, but refused to acknowledge them.  When she reached the safety of her office, she entered and slammed the door shut.  She glanced at the clock on her wall.  Only four hours and eight minutes before the press would be there and she could get the show started.  Until then, she'd amuse herself by reading the Gonzales indictment again.

Harold stood outside Kathy's office door.  He debated whether or not to knock.  After a minute or two, he decided there was no point.  Thelma was dead.  Shannon was dead.  This Carraway woman was fairly new and surely didn't know much about that case that had Mr. Gonzales on edge.  He whipped out his cell phone and dialed quickly.  It rang twice before a gruff voice on the other end answered.

"Mr. Gonzales, I'm here at the DOJ Building in Dallas.  Yes, sir, I know you are getting ready for your swearing in ceremony.  I just wanted to let you know I don't think Miss Carraway is going to present a problem."

"Did you sanitize Ross' office?"

"I sure did, Mr. Gonzales.  Miss Carraway is so caught up in grief right now, it will be a while before she thinks about cases or files or anything else.  I don't think you have anything to worry about."

"I'd better not, or your head will roll."

Then the call disconnected.  In true Alberto Gonzales form, he'd gotten what he needed and then discarded the gift giver.  One day, Karma would surely bite that man in his behind, Harold thought.  He just hoped he'd be around to see it.

For now, he had a little bit of work to do.  He'd work from his laptop in the break room for a while so he wouldn't be in anyone's way.  His car service wouldn't arrive until one in the afternoon to transport him to the airport.  He thought dealing with Miss Carraway and clearing Miss Ross' office was going to take the entire morning.  He was pleasantly surprised it had not.  Aside from a few memos and reports he needed to get done before he arrived back in D.C, he decided to spend his time engaged in a job search.  He was sick of Alberto Gonzales and ready to move on to the next project.  He headed back down the hall to the break room.  When he reached the empty room, he shut the door and put his earbuds in so he could be in his own world and neither disturb or be disturbed.

Several hours passed before a flurry of motion jolted Harold awake. He realized he must have fallen asleep while he worked. He looked at his phone. It was ten minutes before noon. He still had a little time before his car arrived. He decided to follow the activity and see what was going on. He put his laptop away in his computer bag, tossed in his phone, and took one last swig of coffee.

As he entered the hallway, he saw there was far more activity than he realized. Miss Ross had been a prominent community figure, but there were what looked like hundreds of reporters packed shoulder to shoulder, setting up equipment. He looked ahead to the Briefing Room and saw that it, too, was stuffed full of media personnel. He inched down the hall and stopped in front of a window. He'd wait here until the crowd died down. That's when he noticed a sea of reporters outside on the lawn, as well. He'd never met Miss Ross personally, but he figured she must have truly been a pillar in this community, based upon the apparent reaction to her death. He glanced at the clock on the wall across from him. It was exactly noon.

At that moment, Kathy greeted everyone. Television monitors had been placed so that occupants of the entire building, both inside and out, could hear and see Kathy as she spoke. She gave some history on the pay to play scam that permeated the healthcare industry, then she described how illicit drug sales tied in. She talked about the dead Houston attorney and then about Thelma. She detailed the contents of indictments against eighty one individuals. In a climactic final revelation, she discussed how Shannon staged her death in order to reel in the biggest fish of them all: Alberto Gonzales.

She paused briefly for effect, then proceeded to read the indictment against Mr. Gonzales. It contained a total of one hundred thirty six provable offenses.  Even with the best attorney available, Kathy estimated he'd rot behind bars for his despicable ways. She thanked everyone for coming out, then excused herself to her office.  Harold Penigar smiled a crooked smile.  He could hardly contain himself as he looked up and thanked God for allowing him to witness Karma kick his boss in the teeth.

Alberto Gonzales watched from a television in his bedroom in D.C.  He was being sworn in as Attorney General of the United States in two and a half hours.  He'd have to deal with this foolishness later. He picked up the remote to turn his television set off. As he raised it, he saw their reflection on the screen. He dropped the remote and raised his hands.

In the doorway of his bedroom stood more federal agents than he could count.  They were like ants about to pounce collectively on a sugar cube.  There was representation from every agency it seemed, but the FBI took the lead. They all seemed to savor this moment of discomfort he faced.

"I'm the Attorney General of the United States of America! I'll be out before your shift is over."

Several of the FBI agents snickered aloud. The "do you know who I am?" line tended to amuse them when criminals used it. They'd seen the indictments and charge sheets. He'd be going nowhere anytime soon. In light of the latest developments, Ralph Sarazen had been sworn in a half hour earlier as the country's new Attorney General. So, old Alberto no longer had that clout either. He was handcuffed and informed of his rights before being led away to a waiting FBI sedan.

Back in Dallas, Kathy had linked up with "the gang" at Shannon's house for an early dinner. They sat around the dinner table, thankful for  much needed relaxation. They shared their plans. Jake, Penny and Clint had claimed their fourteen million each for services rendered over the last ten years.  Clint and Penny were going to pick up her kids and head to their new ranch in Plano.  Jake had packed bags for himself and his sister.  They had plans for a much needed rest in Hawaii before they gave thought to what would be next.

"Great job, Shannon!" Kathy told her friend, as she stuffed another bite of manicotti in her mouth.

"I couldn't have done it without you.  All of you."

"So, what's next?  Is retirement still on the horizon for you?" Kathy asked.

"Absolutely not."

"Really?  I thought you were looking forward to a slower pace," Kathy chided.

"I decided I can have my cake and eat it, too.  I'll still attend seminary, but I won't quit the DOJ just yet.  I have to stick around for at least another year or two so I can help the new Chief settle in."

"New chief?  Ugh.  I can't deal with a new Chief right now.  I hope they have their act together and aren't a jerk."

"From what I can see, you have your stuff together.  Not sure about the jerk part yet, though."

Kathy froze in place and stared at Shannon. She wasn't sure the implication of what she'd just heard.  She turned to look at her brother. Jake's smile assured her she understood what Shannon just said.

"I knew we should have gotten a bottle of Champagne!" Penny squealed.

This lightened the mood even more.

"Are you sure about this?" Kathy asked Shannon.

"I'm positive.  You have more than earned it."

"I just don't know what to say.  Thank you for having that much confidence in me.  And speaking of 'earned it,' you've earned this."

Kathy held her hand out toward Jake. He reached in his jacket pocket and pulled out an envelope. He handed it to his sister. She placed it on the table in front of Shannon.

"What's this?" Shannon asked.

"Look and see," Kathy urged.

Shannon carefully unsealed the envelope. Inside was a Cashier's Check for three million dollars. One million each from Penny, Clint and Jake.

"I can't accept this. You all sacrificed so much for this," Shannon said.

"So did you," Jake assured her.

"And we have more than enough left to live on. We'll invest wisely and leave some for future generations. If not for you, we wouldn't even have this. After Thelma's death, there was no guarantee of payment. Thanks for making sure we were taken care of," Kathy said, fighting tears of gratitude.

"Well, hurry back from this trip to Hawaii. We have another big case to work on," Shannon lightheartedly ordered.

Then she gave her signature wink. The group burst into a collective laughter, which cleansed their souls and renewed their spirits. They were ready to face whatever life threw at them because they knew they had each other.

## Epilogue

Shannon Ross, Thelma Quince Colbert, Michael Weiss and Alberto Gonzales are all real people.  Shannon Ross was one of the author's college professors in the early 1990s in Dallas, Texas.  Her tough as nails, God fearing, seek justice, love mercy type of personality had a profound impact upon the author of this book.  This book is in tribute to her spirit, though it's a fabricated tale and not a biopic.

This story has elements of non-fiction blurred with fiction, so this story is not real, but many of the nuances are.  Shannon Ross was actually found deceased in her home shortly after signing indictments and securing warrants in the healthcare case in September of 2004.  She was headed toward retirement and planned to attend seminary school at Ft Worth's Texas Christian University. Thelma Quince Colbert was found deceased at her home, in July of 2004, drowned in her swimming pool, while working on the healthcare case.  Houston Attorney Michael Weiss was also found deceased by his housekeeper in October of 1999 after he initiated and pursued litigation in the healthcare scandal.  After Shannon's death, her entire unit was dismantled.  Three attorneys were fired and several others resigned.  The real life New York Times contact of Shannon and Thelma, Mary Williams Walsh, was moved out of judicial reporting and no longer allowed to report on the healthcare story at the same time Shannon's unit was disbanded.  Alberto Gonzales still lives.  Is he a wicked man?  Were his superiors, including the President, wicked?  Were any or all of them involved in one of the biggest scandals of our time?

It's been more than two decades at the time of this book's publication, and no one knows the truth.  The news blackout and lack of investigation, particularly regarding two dead U S Attorneys, has led many to believe foul play was involved.  Research the

facts and see what your own conclusions are.

Michelle enjoys hearing from readers.  You can contact her/give her feedback by emailing her at iinfo@kmpentertainment.org

You can keep up with her projects by going to her company's website www.kmpentertainment.org or via Facebook at the KMP Entertainment page, https://www.facebook.com/KMPEntertainment/

You can find other books written by Michelle by visiting the KMP Entertainment website, Amazon and other retailers.

Another of Michelle's books you are sure to enjoy is THE BURG.  Devi stumbles upon corruption in Oregon  and it takes her on a wild ride that would intimidate most anyone.  Murder, mayhem, collusion, drugs, and more.  She faces what she finds head-on, with no plans to back down.

About the Author:

After a career in the United States Army, Michelle decided to pursue her passions. These include writing, acting, traveling, camping, SCUBA diving, horsemanship, volunteering and spending time with her son, Kendal. Michelle is also an actress, and host of talk radio program, Chelle's Three Cents, on Blogtalkradio. She is the writer and Executive Producer of the KMP production "Mendacity." You may also know her work from shows like "Man With a Plan" on CBS, or "Crazy Ones" with Robin Williams, or other broadcast shows such as The Cleaning Lady. Additionally, she is the 2019 Miss North Hollywood California Plus America title holder. Michelle holds an undergraduate degree in Entertainment Business and a Master of Fine Arts degree in Creative Writing. She is currently pursuing her Doctorate.

www.ingramcontent.com/pod-product-compliance
Lightning Source LLC
Chambersburg PA
CBHW020109310726

48970CB00002B/541